Their eyes l[...] body submitted to an overpowering magnetic pull.

At the sight of Lucius's head descending, the muscles in her belly quivered and her heart pounded so loud she feared the whole world could hear it. When their lips finally made contact, Beverly's eyes fluttered close and once again, she was lost.

However, this time was different. In her mind, not only could she hear music but there was this wonderful floating sensation that made her feel lush and giddy. She pressed closer, greedy for more.

Lucius eagerly gave her what she wanted—what they both wanted. He had spent the evening wondering what she would taste like and he wasn't disappointed. Her lips were amazingly soft and decadently sweet. A man, if he wasn't too careful, could get caught up.

Books by Adrianne Byrd

Kimani Romance

She's My Baby
When Valentines Collide
To Love a Stranger
Her Lover's Legacy
Sinful Chocolate
*Tender to His Touch

*Hollington Homecoming

ADRIANNE BYRD

is a national bestselling author who has always preferred to live within the realms of her imagination, where all the men are gorgeous and the women are worth whatever trouble they manage to get into. As an army brat, she traveled throughout Europe and learned to appreciate and value different cultures. Now, she calls Georgia home.

Ms. Byrd has been featured in many national publications, including *Today's Black Woman, Upscale* and *Heart and Soul.* She has also won local awards for screenwriting.

In 2006 Adrianne Byrd forged into the world of Street Lit as De'nesha Diamond. In 2008 she jumped into the young-adult arena writing as A. J. Byrd, and in 2010 Adrianne will hit the women's fiction scene as Layla Jordan. She plans to continue creating characters that make people smile, laugh and fall in love.

Tender to His Touch
ADRIANNE BYRD

HOLLINGTON HOMECOMING
Where old friends reunite...and new passions take flight

This book is dedicated to: Sandra Kitt, Jacqueline Thomas
and Pamela Yaye. It was a pleasure working with you
talented ladies.

KIMANI PRESS™

Recycling programs
for this product may
not exist in your area.

ISBN-13: 978-0-373-86141-5

Special thanks and acknowledgment to Adrianne Byrd for her
contribution to the Hollington Homecoming miniseries.

TENDER TO HIS TOUCH

Copyright © 2009 by Harlequin Books S.A.

www.kimanipress.com

Printed in U.S.A.

Dear Reader,

Welcome back to Hollington College! This is the final book in this sexy, emotional reunion series. Next up: Beverly Turner and Lucius Gray. As Hollington's class of '99 homecoming queen, Beverly seems to have lived a fairy tale existence. But once she married her college sweetheart, it all turned into a nightmare. Now ten years later, she's looking for a new start and I believe I have just the man for her.

You might want to curl up next to an industrial fan for this one, romantics. You're in for one hot, spicy read as Lucius helps this beauty find her own groove. Maybe there are even a few clues we can all learn from this insatiable couple.

Wishing you the best of love,

Adrianne

Prologue

Beverly Clark's eyes were wide open when her alarm clock blared at five-thirty. She flung out an arm and shut off its loud and annoying buzz. However, she didn't climb out of bed. Instead she remained nestled in her white cotton sheets, staring up at her popcorn ceiling.

She hated that damn ceiling.

It reminded her of cottage cheese or, worse, something she used to study under a microscope in her old science lab class eons ago. One of these days she was going to take Spackle or a chisel to the damn thing and scrape that junk off. Beverly huffed, rolled over onto her side and stared at the clock. Its loud ticking sounded as if it had been hooked up to an amplifier. In no time her heart and the muscles along her temples thumped in precise harmony.

Maybe she should just stay in bed today.

Why not? What difference would it make? It wasn't as if anybody cared—or that she had anything to do.

The numbers on the clock blurred and in the next second warm tears slid from her eyes, rolled down her nose, then dripped quietly onto her pillowcase. She pulled in a deep breath, but her lungs felt as if they were trying to resist being revived. Her shoulders trembled and before long her entire body followed suit. It was five forty-five in the morning and she was crying.

A whole fifteen minutes ahead of schedule.

Reluctantly Beverly peeled the sheets back and pulled herself up. Those two simple acts nearly zapped all her energy. From across the room, she caught sight of herself in the full-length mirror and was repulsed by what she saw.

"Oh, God." She raised a hand to her sunken face while her fingers traced the deep lines below her bloodshot eyes. Her full lips looked bee-stung and cracked, and her hair...well, let's just say that it would probably be easier to cut it than comb it. Her hands fell from her face and slapped against her lap. "Look at what's become of me."

Being the daughter of two prominent doctors, Beverly had grown up in an affluent and privileged life. Friends and family had told her throughout the years that she'd been lucky to have inherited her mother's honey-brown complexion and liquid-gold eyes. In her youth, the combination had made her popular with the opposite sex and garnered more than a few sniping remarks from girls who'd assumed she was stuck-up. Those opinions usually changed, though, once people got to know her.

Beauty and charm helped land her the Miss Georgia Teen crown at sixteen and the Miss Georgia crown at eighteen. Plus she was also homecoming queen in both high school and in college. She was smart, too—at least she liked to think she was. She had managed to graduate in the top of her class and at one time had given serious thought to following her parents' example and enrolling in medical school. But after an art teacher pointed out she had a natural flair for fashion, Beverly started spending hours upon hours daydreaming that one day her fashions would be worn on red carpets around the world.

But love intervened and she ended up marrying her old high-school sweetheart, David Clark, right after college despite the protests of her parents. It didn't matter at the time. Surely her parents could grow to love her husband.

David had been a year older and, once upon a time, more mature. They had been so careful planning out their lives. He'd continued his schooling and become a dentist. It turned out to be a great decision. His career had afforded them a great life in the suburbs, but three years ago it all came crashing to an end.

More tears leaked from Beverly's eyes.

From a distance, a car turned into the driveway. She turned her head toward the open window and listened to the smooth rumble of a Mercedes engine as it coasted toward the house. Beverly wiped her face and reached for her satin robe draped over the foot of her bed.

Beneath the window, the engine shut off, the car door opened and then slammed shut. The familiar footfalls of expensive Ferragamo loafers slapped against the pavement and then up the front porch. Beverly stood when she heard keys rattle in the front-door lock.

Inside the house, the heavy footsteps continued through the foyer and then up the staircase. Beverly tried to mentally prepare herself for her daily battle, but on this day she found that she simply couldn't. She just didn't have anything left.

The knob turned and the bedroom door crept open. David poked his head inside, his attention on the empty bed.

"Glad to see that you found your way home," Beverly said, her wintry voice chilling the room. "And here I thought buying that GPS unit was a complete waste of money."

Unable to hide his disappointment, David released a long, frustrated sigh. "I thought you'd still be asleep."

"I haven't slept in years."

He rolled his eyes and pulled his wrinkled tie from around his neck. "Maybe that's your problem." David headed toward the adjoining bathroom.

"*My problem?*" she said, her eyes narrowing on his retreating back. Beverly followed. "Maybe *my problem* is that my *husband* is out screwing his office manager at all hours of the night while I'm stuck in this suburban prison cooking dinners for one."

"There you go again. No one's screwing around," he said. "And I'm not stopping you from getting out of the house. That's your choice. In fact, I wish you would get out. Maybe the neighbors would stop looking at me as if I've chained you up in the basement or something." He turned on the shower.

"*No one's screwing around,*" she thundered incredulously.

"Do I look stupid to you?" she hissed. "It is six o'clock in the morning. Nearly twelve hours since the office closed *yesterday*. Are you going to tell me that you had some dental emergency that kept you at the office and strategically away from a phone all this time?"

His eyes rolled again as he unbuttoned and then slid out

of his pants. "I went out for a few drinks with the guys. I crashed over at Curtis's place."

David finally stopped and looked at her. Guilt was etched in every inch of his handsome face. The same face that she'd once vowed to love for the rest of her life. She now longed to rake her nails down its gorgeous perfection. Why did it seem as if the nightmare of the last three years had not scared him the way it had her? Why was it so easy for him to just move on? If they were truly soul mates why weren't they living in the same hell?

"What?" David asked defensively.

"If you're going to be a playa, then learn to get your lies straight."

"I told you—"

"Curtis called here last night looking for you. He wanted to know whether you two were still going fishing today."

Thick clouds of steam billowed from the shower, then swirled around the fractured husband and wife. The battle of their heated gazes raged on for a few heartbreaking seconds and then finally, resignation flickered across David's face. He'd been busted and his brain failed to come up with a plausible lie.

"Just admit it," she urged in a thin whisper. She half convinced herself that she would feel better if he'd just confess that he'd been having an affair. Confess that the perfume clinging to his clothes right now wasn't just her imagination.

"Beverly—"

"Say it," she choked out.

"Bev—"

"Goddamn it, *say it!*" She snatched a curling iron from the vanity counter and hurled it at him. The bastard ducked and the curling iron slammed against the glass shower stall. It hit a weak spot and the whole thing shattered as if she had unloaded an AK-47 at it.

David leaped away from the shower as shards of glass launched toward him. "All right! All right! I'm having an affair. Are you happy now?" he roared.

Beverly sucked in a breath and stepped back as if he'd punched her. Her mind reeled. She couldn't decide if she wanted to hit him, scratch him or kick him in the balls.

As he realized what he had said, regret blanketed David's face. He reached for her. "Beverly, I—"

"Don't touch me." She pulled away. "I want you out. Out of this house and out of my life!"

"Look, Beverly. I didn't mean to—"

"It's over." She took another huge step back, shaking her head. "I want a divorce," she said evenly.

He wouldn't give up. "We've been through a lot," he reminded her. "We can get through this."

"No, we can't," she contradicted. "We can't...because I don't love you anymore."

Chapter 1

Two years later

A jacketless and tieless Lucius Gray was nearing his tenth hour poring over documents and case files. He kept telling himself that he'd quit for the day—or rather, night—every ten minutes, but his determination to know this wrongful death case backward and forward prevented him from leaving. He wanted all his ducks in a row so he could squeeze Dr. E. J. Stewart and his insurance company into settling the case for a mid-eight-figure settlement.

It wasn't one of his biggest litigation cases, but this particular case hit him hard. The similarities between Mr. Keith Johnson's death and Lucius's father's were just too striking. Dr. Stewart, a cardiologist, kept finding nothing wrong with Mr. Johnson a year after he had a stint implanted and recommended he see an oncologist for his illness. Of course the oncologist found nothing wrong with him and kept referring him back to his cardiologist. All the while, Mr. Johnson's condition grew worse and worse. When he finally passed away, the autopsy showed that he had a lot of blockages in his arteries and his poor heart just gave out. There were so many of them that it was just unexplainable how Dr. Stewart had missed the obvious.

What did it say about the state of the health-care system when doctors were just too busy to do their jobs?

The phone chirped.

Lucius glanced up, annoyed to have had his concentration broken. He punched the speakerphone button. "Yeah?"

"Mr. Gray, I have your wife on line one."

He frowned. "You mean my *ex*-wife, don't you, Maggie?"

"I'm just repeating what *she* said."

Lucius drew a deep breath and pitched back into his chair. Until that moment, he hadn't noticed how hungry he was or how tight his neck muscles had become.

"Mr. Gray?"

"Put her through," he said and expelled a tired breath. In the next second the phone rang and he picked up. "What can I do for you, Erica?"

"You haven't been able to do anything for me in a loooooonnng time," she answered in her usual sarcastic tone.

He rolled his eyes. "I really don't have time to fight with you right now. So—"

"I know. I know," Erica huffed. "You're working on a really important case. The story of our marriage."

"So you kept reminding me through the divorce." Lucius's office door crept open and he looked up in time to see Maggie poke her head inside. He didn't miss the tired lines beneath her eyes or how her morning curls had wilted on her head. "Erica, hold on for a moment." He hit the phone's mute button without waiting for his ex-wife's permission.

"I'm getting ready to head out," Maggie said. "Is there anything else you need?"

Lucius glanced at his watch. It was well past seven o'clock. "No. I'm good. Have a good night. I'll see you in the morning."

Maggie nodded and then disappeared back behind the door.

Lucius drew a deep breath and hit the mute button again. "I'm back."

"I can't bring Ruby this weekend. It'll have to be next weekend."

Lucius's grip tightened on the phone. In the five years since his divorce, he and Erica kept playing the same game with their now eight-year-old daughter—the emotional blackmail game. And now that Erica had a new man, Andrew, in her life, she seemed steadfastly determined to have this jerk take Lucius's place. "You said that *last* weekend, Erica."

"It was true last weekend, too," Erica snorted. "And don't act like you're so disappointed."

"I made plans," he said, though it wasn't exactly true. He'd planned to wing it. Maybe take Ruby to Chuck E. Cheese or a movie or something.

"Please." He could practically see Erica rolling her eyes. "Buying her a bunch of junk food and dragging her to your office isn't exactly a trip to Disney World."

Great. She played a guilt card. "It was just that one time."

"Uh-huh," she said dubiously. "Like I said, I can't bring her this weekend. Andrew wants to take Ruby up to Boston."

"Boston?" Lucius barked, irritated. "What the hell is in Boston?"

"Andrew is from Boston…and we're going up to meet his family."

Silence.

"Lucius?"

"So…what? This *relationship* is getting serious?" He was surprised by his annoyance.

"Maybe," she hedged, her tone finally softening.

Lucius closed his eyes and then rubbed the tension from his forehead. It wasn't that he still harbored romantic feelings toward his ex-wife. It was more that the threat of him being replaced in Ruby's life with another man was becoming a reality at a pace that made him more than uncomfortable. "C'mon, Erica. How long have you known this guy? Two months—three?"

"A year," she corrected him.

Had a year passed that quickly?

"Of course, if you ever pulled your head out from your…work, you'd see that life was passing you by."

Lucius heaved another frustrated sigh. "Can we not fight tonight? I have a headache."

"Fine."

The line fell silent, but the tension remained. Finally he said, "I don't know if I like this."

Erica chuckled. "Don't tell me that I've finally done something to catch your attention."

"Is that what this is all about—getting my attention?"

Her laugh deepened. "Please. I've stopped trying to do that a long time ago. You made it perfectly clear that your work is all that matters to you."

"That's not true."

"It feels true." Another awkward silence drifted over the line. "I'll bring Ruby next weekend," she said and then disconnected the line.

Lucius held the phone until the automated voice came on and instructed him on how to make a call. "That went well," he mumbled under his breath. He settled back in his chair, replaying the call in his head and wishing he had handled the situation better. But what had been obvious for many years now was, point-blank, he and Erica just rubbed each other the wrong way.

His gaze fell on a framed photograph of his precocious daughter, Ruby. He struggled to remember exactly how old she was in the picture—maybe four or five. It was an adorable picture of her with her thick black hair parted into two fat ponytails. On the day of the picture, she was so proud to show off the loss of her two front teeth. Her big quarter-size hazel eyes danced with excitement at the possibility of seeing the Tooth Fairy.

Lucius reached over his desk and picked up the photograph. Instantly, his irritation and annoyance at Erica melted away and a broad smile broke across his face. Ruby was a perfect amalgam of him and Erica. She had his warm brown complexion and hazel eyes and Erica's button nose and full lips. "Daddy's little girl," he whispered, feeling his chest swell with pride.

Ruby Elizabeth Gray was the absolute joy of his life— despite what her mother thought. Sure, he had been thrown out of his element from time to time by tea parties with imaginary guests or playing baby dolls with dolls that actually did number one *and* number two. However, most of that came from the fact Lucius grew up in a family dominated by men.

It had been a real shock to him when the doctor told him and Erica that they were going to have a girl. He didn't know what to do with a girl. Up until that ultrasound, he had envisioned mock football and basketball games with *Junior.* Instead he got a little girl that stole his heart like no other. And he was a better man for it.

Lucius slowly rocked his neck from side to side, but his tense muscles refused to relax and his empty stomach rumbled in protest. Sighing with regret, he knew that it was finally time to call it a night. Propelling out of his chair, he quickly stuffed the case files into his briefcase, slid on his office jacket and crammed his tie into his pocket.

As he exited the building of Kendall, Hendrix and Gray, LLC, he contemplated which fast-food drive-through he was in the mood for. Once behind the wheel of his black Cadillac SRX Crossover, he elected instead to finish off some leftovers he had back at the crib. He'd always been careful to take care of his body through regular exercise and a healthy diet, and there was no need to wreck all that for a greasy burger.

It was well past eight o'clock by the time he finally pulled into his large two-car garage. As usual when he headed toward the garage door that led into the kitchen, he tossed a longing look toward his old wood workshop. His *man* space, as Erica used to call it. How long had it been now since he'd lost himself in the hobby of building things—six years...seven?

He had always enjoyed working and making things with his hands. It had a way of relaxing him. However, with the influx of bank and credit fraud, his law firm had enjoyed a healthy spike in litigation and court cases. There just hadn't been any time to whittle the hours away in his workshop.

Soon, he promised himself. He'd make the time one day soon.

Lucius entered the house, flipped on the light switch, placed his briefcase on the counter and made a beeline toward the refrigerator. Thirty minutes later he was settled at the dinner table and casually sifting through the day's mail. He stopped when he came across the envelope from Hollington College.

His smile was instant. "Hollington." He chuckled, opening the envelope. "My old stomping grounds." Suddenly memories of football and frat parties filled his head, as well as the small string of college shawties he'd juggled while struggling to maintain his high GPA.

"'October homecoming weekend,'" he read. His eyes quickly scanned over the invitation card. "Tenth anniversary? Has it been that long already?" He shook his head. Where had all the time gone? Thinking about it, a lot had happened in ten years: marriage, law school, law practice, a baby, working like hell, making partner, working like hell, divorce, working like hell.

There was a theme in there somewhere.

"All work and no play make Lucius a dull man," he whispered. He glanced up and truly took stock of the empty dining-room chairs surrounding the table. Outside, the evening crickets played their songs while his expensively furnished house felt awfully cold…and lonely.

His gaze shifted back to the invitation. Maybe this was exactly what he needed. A little time out with some old friends…and old girlfriends.

"Beverly, what do you mean you're not going to the reunion?" Kyra asked, her hands propped on her slender hips. "This is a big weekend for the university and I'm counting on you to be there."

"I don't see why," Beverly said, straightening a rack of embellished skirts. Her trendy, high-end boutique, Hoops, was on North Highland Avenue and a steady stream of twentysomethings flowed into the store and left carrying enormous white shopping bags with the dainty Hoops logo. The sparkly chandelier, golden cherubs and tasteful furniture lent a chic, intimate feel to the place. "Aside from you and a couple of other people, I haven't kept in touch with anyone from our graduating class."

"Beverly, you were homecoming queen and everyone's expecting you to be there."

"That's too bad, because I'm not going."

"Give me one good reason why you can't go."

"I'll give you three. For starters, I'm swamped here." Selecting a dazzling sheath from off the rack, she slipped it off the gold, padded hanger and held it up to one of the mannequins in the front window. "I'm putting together the final touches for my new spring line, and I have to design a gown for Gabrielle Union to wear to an awards gala next month."

"You seem stressed, Bev. Why don't you let me take you out for lunch?"

"So you can pressure me into going to the reunion?" Beverly shook her head. "No way. I don't have time for this right now. I'm up to my neck in paperwork and it's going to take me the rest of the afternoon to fill the online orders."

"Beverly, you've been dodging my calls for weeks and the reunion is less than a month away. I need to help finalize the rest of the plans for homecoming."

She said nothing, just continued dressing the mannequin

and humming to the Smokey Robinson song playing in the background.

Kyra heaved a heavy sigh. "So, that's it? You're not going and there's nothing I can say or do to change your mind?"

Beverly gave a brisk nod, and then changed the subject. "I was at my favorite fabric store last week and it seemed the whole town was abuzz with the news of Terrence's big return."

"Yeah, his arrival has generated a lot of good press for the school. We're received hundreds of online applications, and we had so much traffic on the Web site yesterday, it crashed!"

"I bet," Beverly agreed. "After all, he is the pride of Hollington."

"I'm lining up as many interviews as I can. I even contacted my old sorority sister, Tamara Hodges, about doing an article on Terrence becoming the Lions' coach."

Her eyebrows rose. "You got him to sign on already?"

"Not yet, but I will."

Beverly started to speak, but her words were drowned out by a shrill, piercing laugh. Realizing they needed privacy, Kyra grabbed Beverly's hand and dragged her into the back office. While the boutique was bright and glitzy, the office was a simple, understated space teeming with fashion magazines, invoices and poster boards. "Now," Kyra began, closing the door and standing in front of it, "spill it. What's the real reason you won't go to the reunion?"

Beverly stood her ground. "You're not going to change my mind, so you might as well save your breath."

"The class of ninety-nine voted *you* homecoming queen, Beverly. How's it going to look if you don't show up?"

"Like I'm a popular fashion designer who has orders to fill." Straightening up, she folded her arms across her chest, her gaze drifting to the open window. "Kyra, I'm not trying to be difficult, but I've moved on from beauty pageants and modeling contests. I want to be taken as a serious business-woman and that's not going to happen if I'm riding on top of a flowered float."

In an effort to keep the peace, Kyra listened to what she had to say without interrupting. Beverly was frowning, and she could tell by the faraway look in her eyes that her mind was somewhere else. "Why does it feel like you're blowing me off?"

"I'd never do that," Beverly insisted, shaking her head. "We're friends, remember?"

"Then can a sister get a discount on that gold Ferra-gamo gown?"

Beverly gave a brief sputter of laughter.

"Hanging out with old friends is just what you need. You've been divorced for almost two years, but you haven't been on a single date. I'm not telling you to go out there and party like Paris Hilton, but live a little, girl! Go to the reunion, and have a good time. And if you see someone who catches your eye…" Kyra trailed off, her glossy red lips curling into a mischievous smirk. "There are going to be plenty of handsome, eligible brothers at the reunion, Bev. It would be a shame for you to miss out."

A smile broke through. "You must be very good at your job," she teased.

"I try," Kyra sang, laughing. Sensing a subtle shift in her friend's mood, and anxious to get her on board, she con-tinued, "Homecoming weekend is your opportunity to shine. Do you know how much business you'll drum up for the boutique just by being there wearing one of your gorgeous, one-of-a-kind creations?"

"I never even thought of that. It would be great for business, wouldn't it?"

Kyra nodded. "How about I contact Tamara and ask her to do a piece in *Luster* about Hoops? It's free publicity and last year the magazine surpassed *Glamour* magazine in sales."

"I'll think about it."

"Oh, you're going, all right," Kyra vowed, lobbing an arm around Beverly's shoulders, "because I won't take no for an answer!"

That was exactly what Beverly was afraid of.

Chapter 2

"Girrrrl, you are going to get laid for sure in that dress." Clarence, Beverly's best friend and self-appointed relationship advisor, snapped his fingers and twirled her around so she could face the full-length mirror.

A cocky grin sloped across Beverly's face. She did look good. The red cocktail dress hugged her curvy body like an extra layer of skin and she debated whether she even needed the thin silver belt. What was even more surprising was how much she loved her new hairstyle.

Clarence switched his hips and smacked his clear, shimmering lips. "Do I know how to hook my girl up or what?"

Beverly happily agreed. The shorter, darker do made her golden eyes pop and easily erased the past ten years from her face. She might actually pull this off.

"Now remember, whatever booty you get, fifteen percent of it is mine."

Beverly howled and then bumped her hip against his. "What the hell am I going to do with you?"

"Love me, sweetheart. That's what they all do with me." He leaned forward and blew air kisses. Dressed in an immaculate pair of shiny denim jeans and a cloud-white shirt beneath a black merino sweater, Clarence was as sharp as any male model strutting down a Prada runway. On his youthful, effeminate face he wore the lightest touch of face powder and lip gloss.

"Well, I better go," Clarence said as he turned away from the mirror and marched out of the bathroom. "It's Friday night and you're not the only bitch trying to get laid."

Beverly laughed as she followed. "Thanks again, Clarence. I don't know what I would have done if you didn't come over."

"Uh-huh." Clarence glanced around the large hotel suite, specifically the huge king-size bed.

"Look, I'm just staying here at the hotel during homecoming weekend because it's a lot closer to Hollington College than my house. If I happened to have a few drinks, it's easier to catch a cab here than risk driving all the way back out to the suburbs."

Clarence wasn't buying it. "Whatever, chickie." He switched his hips as he retrieved his jacket. "You just make sure this big ol' bed doesn't go to waste this weekend. I've been telling you you needed to get your groove back for a while. I'm glad Kyra finally brought you around."

Beverly actually blushed. "I never said I was going to this homecoming to get laid."

"Uh-huh." Clarence popped his lips.

"I came to just have a good time and catch up with old friends." The lie even sounded weak to her.

Clarence rolled his eyes. "Girl, I know a freakum dress when I see it." He headed to the door. "Have a good time and I expect details when I come by Hoops next week."

Beverly chuckled and then added, "Thanks again for coming to my hair emergency. I was ready to pack up and go back home."

"Relax." Clarence reached over and squeezed her hand. "You're the homecoming queen. They're going to love you. And *if* that jerk of an ex-husband of yours does show up, give him a good swift kick in the balls for me."

Lucius was getting excited at the thought of returning to his old stomping grounds. Rumors had been circulating that both Terrence Franklin and Micah Ross would be swinging through the joint. He hoped to get a little face time with his old buddies and shoot the breeze. He had only one last business errand to run over at the downtown Hilton before he headed off to the college. Once he dropped off a few documents with one of his clients, he promised himself to turn off his BlackBerry and just enjoy his weekend.

Hell, he deserved it.

However, Atlanta's Friday bumper-to-bumper traffic delayed his plans for a carefree weekend. While surrounding cars engaged in an endless game of cutting each other off, honking and tossing a few middle fingers in the air, Lucius slipped in his old *The Miseducation of Lauryn Hill* CD. Ten years ago, his senior year in college, this disc stayed on repeat. His boys loved it and, more importantly, so did the ladies.

When his favorite jam, "Ex-Factor," came on, a broad smile carved across his lips as he bobbed his head. This was just what he needed to get in the '99 mood. An hour later, he finally arrived at the Hilton and met businessman Mitch Paulson in the hotel bar.

"Ah, right on time," Paulson said as he stood to shake Lucius's hand. "Can I get you a drink?" He waved and caught a waitress's attention.

Lucius glanced at his watch. "Actually, I—"

"Ah, c'mon." Paulson gestured for him to take a seat. "It's the least I can do after having you deliver those papers on such short notice."

Lucius hesitated, glanced at his watch. No way would he make it over to Cork for the school's private cocktail party on time. Then again, maybe it was better to show up fashionably late.

"Don't be rude, Lucius. Have a seat," Paulson insisted and then added a boisterous laugh. "You know businessmen don't like drinking alone."

Lucius relented with a chuckle. "Maybe just one drink."

Their waitress popped up the moment Lucius took his seat. "Whiskey on the rocks," he ordered.

"Make that two," Paulson corrected, giving the pixie blonde a flirtatious wink.

However, the waitress's blue gaze was busy assessing Lucius. She was cute, but Lucius would most likely always crave the touch and love of a curvy sistah. That was just how he rolled.

When the waitress saw that she wasn't getting any play, she drifted away from the table.

"Ah, well," Paulson huffed and reached inside his jacket and retrieved a cigar case. "I guess I'm losing my touch."

Or you shouldn't try to pick up someone young enough to be your granddaughter.

"Just as well, I suppose. It's not easy keeping up with

these young girls," he said, laughing at his own joke. "I damn near threw my back out last year with an eighteen-year-old hell-bent on turning me into a pretzel."

Lucius laughed along, though he picked up on a few notes of sadness.

"Who knows? I probably should've stayed married," Paulson continued. "But…well, back when I was your age I was married to my job more than I was to Sheila."

This always happened when Lucius shared drinks with his male clients. Alcohol loosened tongues and Lucius found himself cast in the role of a pseudopsychiatrist.

"You married, Lucius?" Paulson asked just as their waitress returned with their drinks.

"Divorced."

"Hmmph." Paulson shook his head. "Big mistake."

"I don't know. It seemed to have worked out for the best."

"Sure you say that *now*. Let a few more years roll by." He took a sip of his drink. "Seeing anybody?"

Lucius shifted in his chair as he took a few sips of his whiskey. "Let's just say that I'm keeping my options open."

"How many hours are you putting in at the firm?"

"What is this, an interrogation?"

"Let me guess," Paulson went on, sizing him up. "You look like a workaholic. I'd say about 85 to 90?"

Their gazes locked.

"I'm right, aren't I?" Paulson flashed him a lopsided grin. "Tell me. Have you noticed how cold a house gets at night yet?"

Lucius didn't answer.

"Hmmph." Paulson shook his head. "Believe me. It gets a lot colder. Thing is, I don't ever remember it being that way when I was married. A house is meant to be a home."

He leveled his gaze back on Lucius. "And man was never meant to be alone—that's the one passage I remember from the Bible."

Lucius quickly took another sip of his drink.

"A career is great, but a good woman is even better." Paulson scanned the room. "Are you a breast or leg man?"

"I, uh—"

"Aww. Maybe you like a woman with a little junk in the trunk?" He winked.

Lucius would never get used to old white men trying to talk hip. "Yeah. I guess you can say that I like it all."

Paulson's drink stopped midway to his lips. "Then it looks like you're in luck. Check out who just walked through the door."

Curious, Lucius turned around and nearly dropped his glass when his gaze zeroed in on a tall, gorgeous woman in red with deep brick-house curves and a smile that lit up the whole room. Spellbound, he watched her as she strolled over to the bar. Her big breasts sat high and were like—*pow!* Her firm, but still bouncing backside was like—*ka-pow!*

To maintain some semblance of cool, Lucius sipped a little more of his whiskey, but his eyes never left the seductive sway Paulson so elegantly called *junk in the trunk*.

"Better close your mouth and go make a move," Paulson chuckled. "I'd say you have about five seconds before someone else beats you to the punch."

Lucius tossed down the rest of his drink in one gulp and sprang out of his chair without a backward glance. Halfway over to the bar, he realized that he didn't have the slightest idea what to say. His pickup lines were a little rusty.

Across the room, he saw another brother stand up; his eyes locked on the same mysterious woman. Lucius picked up his pace and settled onto the empty stool beside the lady in red, whose soft floral perfume worked like an invisible hook. Before he could speak, she glanced over her shoulder and smiled.

"Hello," she greeted in a velvety smooth voice that dripped with sin.

Lucius responded with the first thing that popped into his head. "Marry me?"

Chapter 3

Beverly laughed. The question had been so unexpected that she couldn't do anything but. The handsome stranger next to her joined in. His intriguing hazel eyes were so bewitching her heart skipped a beat. She estimated him to be six-two, lean but well muscled. His medium-brown skin had a healthy glow, and he had short-cropped hair that was well-groomed. She fought the sudden impulse to run her fingers through it to see if it was as soft as it looked. Bottom line, he was a good-looking man with a smile that took her breath away.

"Okay. I admit that was a pretty cheesy pickup line," the handsome devil admitted.

"But very effective," she said, throwing him a bone. "Maybe I should be asking how many wives you have stashed away."

He held up his bare right hand. "I'm as free as a bird."

She arched a brow at him. Did he think a missing ring meant anything these days?

"I'm divorced."

"What a coincidence," she said.

"Now what idiot let *you* go?" he countered, shaking his head and hitting her with his sexy dimples.

"I know, right?"

They laughed.

"Mind if I buy you a drink?" he asked.

"Well, I don't—"

"C'mon. Just one."

The bartender popped up out of nowhere.

"What'll you have?" her handsome admirer asked.

"Whoooo, boy. It's, um, been a while." She hesitated, not knowing what to order. She was more of a wine connoisseur and didn't know any of the latest cool alcoholic concoctions so she stuck with an old staple. "I'll just have a Long Island iced tea."

"And I'll have another whiskey on the rocks," the stranger said and then turned his attention back to Beverly. "By the way, I'm Lucius Gray." He extended his hand.

"Beverly Clark—well, Turner, actually." She laughed at the slip. "I can't believe I still make that mistake."

When his large hand closed around hers, a delicious warmth raced up her arm, her nipples hardened and she tingled in places she'd long forgotten about. That was definitely a good sign.

"If you don't mind, I have a second cheesy line I'd like to ask you," Lucius said.

"All right." She smiled. "Shoot."

"What's a beautiful woman like you doing in a bar like this?"

"Well, I just wanted to grab a quick drink to help me relax before I head out for the evening."

His gaze roamed over her. "So you're staying at the hotel?"

The bartender returned. "One Long Island iced tea and one whiskey on the rocks. Enjoy."

Lucius waited patiently for an answer while Beverly took a sip of her drink.

"Mmmm. Now that hit the spot."

He chuckled, deciding to keep an obvious sexual retort to himself.

Beverly glanced over at him and read him easily. "Get your mind out of the gutter."

Lucius held up his hand. "I don't know what you're talking about."

"Yeah, right." She sipped more of her drink. "And to your previous question, I'm just staying at the hotel for the weekend. And yourself?"

"No, I actually, uh—" he glanced around "—had a meeting with a client, but it looks like that's already ended."

"I'm not keeping you from your work, am I?"

"No. No. It's all right." He flashed another smile. "We had already wrapped things up. When you strolled in and caught every brotha's attention in that knockout dress."

"What—this old thing?"

Lucius laughed.

She bobbed her head and then returned to nursing her drink. "So what do you do, Mr. Gray?"

"I'm an attorney…and please, call me Lucius."

"Okay, Lucius," she said, purposely lowering her voice. "It sort of sounds like luscious."

Lucius's eyes darkened with unmistakable desire. "You

can call me that if you like," he said, leaning in close. "But *only* when we're alone."

At the feel of his warm breath against her cheek, Beverly experienced a few more tingles. *Good Lord, one drink and she was ready to jump the man's bones.*

"Anyway," Lucius said, "I work for one of the largest African-American law firms in Atlanta. We primarily deal with big litigation cases. You know, health care, pharmaceuticals and insurance fraud."

"Ahh, an attorney," she said noncommittally.

"What? Don't tell me that you have something against lawyers?"

She shrugged. "No. It's just that…well…"

"What?"

"It's just that you might be the first attorney I actually like."

Lucius choked on his drink. When he recovered, he barked with laughter.

Beverly chuckled at his side. "No offense," she added. "But the last time I had to deal with attorneys I was going through a pretty messy divorce."

"No offense taken, I assure you. And to be completely honest with you, I wasn't too crazy about my divorce attorney, either. If you don't mind my asking, how long ago did you get your freedom papers?"

She shrugged. "Two years."

"Ah. So your wounds are still fresh."

Was he suggesting that she still had baggage? "What about you?"

Lucius took another sip of his drink. "Five years. I've officially been divorced longer than I was married. But I did get a beautiful daughter out of the deal."

Beverly's easy smile dimmed as she reached for her glass.

Lucius soaked in her profile. "Are you sure that we haven't met somewhere before?"

This time, she nearly choked on her drink. "Cheesy line number three," she said, dabbing her mouth with a cocktail napkin.

His laughter deepened as he shook his head. "Nah. Nah. I mean it. You look very familiar to me. Do you live here in Atlanta or did you fly in on business?"

"No. I live here in Atlanta," she said. Her face continued to warm beneath the intensity of his gaze. It didn't help that the alcohol from her drink felt as if it suddenly had a direct pipeline to her blood system. "Mmm." She closed her eyes and enjoyed the small buzz.

Lucius's body reacted to her sexy moan. "Damn. I should've had what you're having."

Beverly giggled—something she hadn't done in a long time.

"So what is it that *you* do, Ms. Turner?"

"I'm a fashion designer—local. I own a boutique out in Virginia Highland. Have you ever been out there?"

He thought hard and long about it. "Can't say that I have." His eyes narrowed. "But I swear you seem familiar. Maybe with lighter hair?"

Beverly blinked. "Actually, I recently darkened it."

He continued to scrutinize. "Was it longer, too?"

"Yes!" Now she tried to study him. Had they met before?

"I'm going to figure it out," he assured her. His eyes continued to roam hungrily.

He wanted to taste a sample of her lips, not doubting for a moment that they would be sweet, intoxicating and downright addictive. He had a nearly uncontrollable desire to bury himself in the soft curves of her body. Good Lord, he was already thinking about her this way after just talking to her for a few minutes. How long had it been since he'd been with a woman? He frowned, trying to come up with an answer. Ten months. Eleven months. A year? Surely, it couldn't have been that long—had it?

He reached for his drink again while trying to rein in his horny body. Hell, if he stood up right now he would have to figure out a way to walk with three legs.

Beverly glanced at her watch.

Lucius did the same. He was *really* going to be late to the private cocktail party. But if he played his cards right, maybe the night would end on a higher note than trying to see how many of his old college buddies still had a head full of hair.

"Can I get you anything else?" the bartender popped up to ask.

Beverly warred with whether she should stick around and enjoy Mr. Lucius's company or get her butt over to Cork for the Hollington private cocktail party. It wasn't any easy decision. It felt good to have a man look at her the way he did. It made her feel beautiful, desired, and downright horny. When was the last time that happened? In her mind, she was already experimenting with different acrobatic positions and she could feel herself overheating.

Whooooaaa, Beverly. Slow it down.

"Are you blushing?" he asked.

"Huh? What? No!" She blinked and shook her head clear of those naughty thoughts. "I'll just have some water," she said.

"Yes, ma'am. Coming right up."

Lucius's evenly groomed brows rose in mild curiosity.

"A woman must know her limitations," Beverly said,

meeting his gaze. "I don't want to do anything I might regret in the morning."

He clearly caught her meaning and licked his lips. "I don't know about regret, but maybe you should do something you'll *enjoy*."

Their eyes locked and the temperature in the bar skyrocketed. *Where was that damn water?*

"Here you go," the bartender said, helping Beverly break the spell she'd fallen under.

"Thank you." She tossed down half its contents in one long gulp.

"Damn. Thirsty?" Lucius asked.

"Just a little." She chuckled.

They glanced at their watches again.

"Am I keeping you from something?"

She hesitated and then gave him an apologetic smile. "I am supposed to be somewhere."

"Oh?"

"It's a cocktail party over at Cork. I—"

Lucius snapped his fingers. "*That's* where I know you from."

Beverly frowned.

"Class of '99. Hollington College. You're *that* Beverly Turner." He balled his hand in front of his mouth and laughed. "You were homecoming queen."

Stunned, Beverly blinked at him. "You graduated at Hollington?"

"Sure did. Four of the best years of my life. Now it's coming back to me." He laughed. "You used to hang with Kyra Dixon, right?"

"Yeah." She continued to struggle to place his face.

"I used to be on the football team with Terrence Franklin. Offensive lineman."

Beverly experienced a flicker of a memory—tall boy, tight ass, hazel eyes. "I think I do remember you," she said, smiling. "What a coincidence."

"I'd say." His smoldering gaze roamed over every inch of her. "Boy, you're just as beautiful today as you were back then."

Beverly's blush deepened. "I love it when a man lies to me."

"We never officially met back then," Lucius confessed. "But I remember peeping you out on more than one occasion." He set down his drink. "Tell you what. Since I'm heading to Cork myself, what do you say I give you a lift?"

It wasn't exactly smart to jump in a car with a man she hardly knew.

He leaned forward and gave her a wink. "I promise, I'm harmless—despite my being a lawyer." He stood from his stool, tossed a few bills onto the bar and then offered her his arm. "C'mon. Live a little."

Beverly could almost hear Clarence cussing her out if she turned down this fine brotha. It would be nice to actually walk into Cork on a handsome man's arm. Plus, who knows how the rest of the night might end up?

Girrrrl, you are going to get laid for sure.

She certainly hoped so. "All right. Let's go."

Chapter 4

Beverly felt wicked as she allowed Lucius to escort her to his car. It had been years since she'd allowed a man to pick her up in a bar. In fact, she would have to think back to all those wild college spring breaks when she'd been so daring. She kept waiting for her conscience to kick in, for reason to stop her from jumping into this man's car; however, that little voice never came. Instead, desire and lust seized her body, making her willing to see just how this whole night would play out.

"After you," Lucius said, opening the passenger door.

Her gaze locked onto his and caused another spark of electricity to flow between them. "Thank you." Slowly, she dipped into the seat.

Lucius closed the door and rushed around to the driver's side. "I can't believe that I'm actually escorting the homecoming queen," he chuckled, gliding into his own seat.

"Oh, please. Don't go on about that." She rolled her eyes. "That was a very long time ago."

He strapped on his seat belt. "But you're riding in the parade Sunday, right?"

"Unfortunately." Beverly sighed and wondered once again how Kyra had talked her into wearing that godforsaken crown and waving to the crowd. In her opinion, there was nothing worse than an aging beauty queen trying to recapture her youth. Back in the day, she thought nothing of pursuing all those titles—heck, there was good scholarship money attached to those pageants. Now that she was older, she just found the whole thing…silly.

She chuckled. Those were those same words her father used to use. He never once liked the idea of her trotting before a phalanx of judges, normally in a skimpy bathing suit, to be judged. It was sort of funny that it had taken her so long to finally agree with him.

Lucius started the car and Lauryn Hill's "Ex-Factor" poured out of the speakers.

"Oh, I love this song," Beverly gasped. "I used to blast it all time back in the day." She rocked in her seat and cooed the lyrics to the song.

Lucius laughed and bobbed his head. "Not bad," he praised. "Baby girl got skills."

"I can hold a note or two." Beverly turned down the volume. "Good enough for car concerts only."

"You're selling yourself too short." He hit her with another deep-dimpled grin that had her feeling as if she was sitting next to a childhood crush. There was no explanation for why she reacted the way she did to him. She had known plenty of good-looking men in her life. A lot of them were confident achievers, too, but Lucius…he had this whole other vibe going. It was this whole sexy-cool thing that had her hanging on his every word—even when he said something cheesy.

A few minutes later, they arrived at Cork—a posh wine bar in downtown Atlanta. The place was so packed that they had to drive around a couple of times before he discovered one parking place in the back of the building. On the outside, the place looked small and quaint, but once inside it was a large open space with dark wood floors. Wine barrels lined one wall while another entire wall was a large mahogany bar behind which were rows and rows of wine bottles.

Tall tables and stools were located off to the sides, leaving the center open for mingling. Soft piano music filtered from hidden speakers and the lighting was somewhat subdued, giving the place a warm, sexy vibe that Beverly was really feeling.

"This is nice," she commented, glancing around. Everyone looked beautiful in their fancy cocktail dresses and casual suits.

"Beverly? Is that you?"

Beverly turned to see a gaggle of women quickly surround her.

"I don't believe it! Look at you. You look beautiful," the leader of the pack exclaimed, taking Beverly by the shoulders and literarily forcing her to do a pirouette.

Beverly beamed a smile at the woman, but after scanning her memory bank, she was unable to place the woman's face with a name. *This is starting to become a trend,* she noted. "Why, thank you," she said when the woman finally released her. "It's so good to see you. How are you doing?" Maybe if she kept the woman talking, she'd be able to figure out who she was.

"Doing good. Just landed a morning spot on CNN and—" she flashed her diamond ring "—married to Damon Woods. Eight years and still going strong." She laughed and batted her long faux lashes. But it was how her voice squeaked and skipped that finally made Beverly clue in to whom she was speaking with. *Darcy Knight*—which meant that the three women flanking her were Kitty Kirkland, Natalie Coles and Keri Evans.

Instantly, a few inches were shaved off Beverly's smile. She and Darcy had an unspoken rivalry back in college *and* high school. It was nothing that was perpetuated on Beverly's end, but Darcy lost both homecoming queen titles to Beverly, as well as placing second in the Ms. Georgia Teen and Ms. Georgia pageants. When they weren't competing, Darcy chased after David like a bitch in heat and she was constantly biting Beverly's look from hairstyles to clothes.

Unfortunately, it didn't look as if the past ten years had been particularly easy on her. At a cursory glance, Darcy's yaki weave didn't exactly match her unrelaxed crown, plus she had on way too much makeup and she'd easily gained fifty pounds. And her happy clique suffered the same fate.

"Is this one of your creations? I heard you were a fashion designer now," Darcy asked, acid dripping from her voice.

"Why, yes. It is. Do you like it?"

"It's…*cute*," Darcy drawled. "You know I thought about going into the fashion biz, too, but I much prefer to work in something a little more *serious*."

Beverly blinked, but before she had the chance to respond to that backhand slap, Darcy changed the subject. "So how's David?" Darcy asked, casting a curious look over at Lucius. "Word is you two tied the knot right after college."

"We did," she confirmed. "And now we're divorced."

Darcy and her gang's faces collapsed in mock sympathy. "Oh, I'm sooo sorry to hear that," Darcy said. "Of course, I always thought that you two were an odd fit."

Her girls bobbed their heads in agreement.

Beverly tensed, but then to her surprise, Lucius wrapped a supporting arm around her waist. She looked up into his smoldering hazel eyes while he smiled down at her.

"David's loss is *my* gain," he told the women without breaking eye contact with Beverly.

She smiled. *Talk about a knight in shining armor.*

Kitty, Natalie and Keri sighed while Beverly swore her body was slowly melting in Lucius's arms. This was the closest they had been tonight; it was almost like being wrapped in a cocoon where she detected the faint scent of his aftershave mixed with his sinfully sexy cologne.

"Aren't you Lucius Gray?" Darcy asked, stepping closer.

"Guilty," he said, finally turning to look at Darcy. "And you are?"

"Darcy Woods—well, it used to be Knight." Her smile was suddenly bright enough to rival the sun. "We met once at a, um…frat party." She twirled a few strands of her hair around her fingers.

Beverly tensed as jealousy pricked her skin. Had Lucius and Darcy had a fling back in the day? One look and she could tell he was wondering the same thing.

"Well, I did attend my fair share of those," he admitted.

"Mmm-hmm." Darcy smiled like a sly cat with a secret. "At this particular party you had quite a bit to drink and I seem to remember you losing a bet to Terrence Franklin and you and Thomas Barrett had to shave your heads and streak through the center of campus."

"Hey," Beverly said, turning. "I remember that!" Her eyes widened, mainly because that night one of the boys shocked the crowd by being *extremely* well-endowed.

Lucius's face darkened to a deep cranberry. "Ah. *That* night. Not exactly one of my most sober decisions."

"Well," Darcy said, swinging her gaze back to Beverly with contempt clearly written on every inch of her face, "looks like your lucky streak continues."

Lucky? Beverly almost laughed in the woman's face. There were plenty of ways to describe her, especially since she'd left college, and lucky wasn't one of them. "I'd thank you not to presume you know anything about my life."

"Hmmph. Well," Darcy said as if she was suddenly bored, "it was good seeing you again. I'm sure that we'll have time to play catch-up later." She blew Beverly a quick air kiss and then ushered her three-ring circus away.

Beverly shook her head, stunned by how the more things changed, the more they stayed the same.

"That was…interesting," Lucius said, glancing back down at her. "How come I get the feeling that you two weren't *really* friends?"

"Picked up on that, did you?"

He chuckled. "How about I get us a drink? You look as if you could use one."

She could, actually. "Thanks."

"Be right back." He winked.

The moment his arm fell from her waist, Beverly's body ached for its return. Again, a strange response to a man she hardly knew.

"There you are!" Kyra threaded her way through a throng of people and then popped up in front of Beverly and wrapped her in a brief hug. "You came."

"As promised," Beverly said, smiling.

"Good." Krya looped her arm through Beverly's. "Please tell me you're having a good time."

"So far so good." She bobbed her head. "Except when I ran into Darcy Knight."

"Oh!" Krya rolled her eyes. "I was hoping her invitation got lost in the mail."

"It's all right. We kept the claws in…kind of."

Kyra's smile exploded. "See. I knew that you could handle yourself. By the way, I love the new haircut and color."

Beverly beamed. "Thanks, I had Clarence hook me up. I swear the man has magic hands when it comes to my hair."

"Well, I think you look beautiful. In fact, you look like you're positively glowing."

Beverly's gaze skittered across the room to the bar, where Lucius scanned a wine menu. "Can I ask you a question?"

"Sure."

"Do you remember a Lucius Gray?" The minute she asked the question she noted a visible change in her friend's face.

"I, uh, yeah…used to play on the football team, I believe. Why?"

Beverly took another cursory glance toward the bar, but noticed Lucius was gone.

"And here we go," Lucius said, suddenly appearing at her side and handing her a glass of red wine. "I hope you like pinot noir," he added, chuckling and circling his arm back around her waist.

Kyra's eyes widened. "You…two…know…each… other?"

Lucius turned and hit Kyra with one of his sexy deep-dimple grins. "Well, I don't believe it. Kyra. Kyra Dixon." He eased from Beverly's side to sweep a startled Kyra into a brief hug. "Don't you look lovely as ever?" He glanced around. "Is Terrence here, too? I can't wait to see him and play catch-up."

Kyra stiffened. "I don't know how you could miss him. He's over there with his big adoring fan club."

Lucius's brows lifted at her tone.

Kyra smiled weakly. "Um, can you two excuse me? I need to go check on something."

Before Beverly or Lucius could respond, she jetted away from their small circle and disappeared into the crowd.

"Was it something I said?" Lucius asked.

Beverly shook her head. "No. It's…a long story."

He clearly picked up the hint and let the subject drop. Minutes later, Beverly and Lucius maneuvered through the crowd like a seasoned couple saying their hellos and reconnecting with old friends. Whenever anyone questioned how long she and Lucius had been dating, no one believed that they had only known each other a few hours. In some respects, even Beverly couldn't believe it. There was definitely a connection between them. The only question was: what were they going to do about it?

"Good evening, everyone. Welcome to Hollington's annual homecoming weekend, and the tenth anniversary of class of ninety-nine," greeted a voice over the microphone. "I'm Kevin Stayton…"

That was as far as he got before the room erupted into shouts and applause. Even Kevin seemed caught off guard by the response. He quickly put up his hand to quiet the group down and regain control.

"Thanks for that, but the reason why I commandeered the mike from President Morrow is to make sure that everyone is made aware of who is responsible for the important and complex job of organizing this weekend. As it turned out, the best person possible was selected. And she's one of ours, class of '99, y'all!"

There was enthusiastic applause until Kevin again signaled for quiet.

"Typical of her, and some of you will remember this from our undergraduate years, she doesn't like drawing attention to herself. She works quietly behind the scenes but she gets the job done, as all of you will experience during the course of this weekend. Ladies and gentlemen, Chloe Jackson!"

Chloe didn't move, and then someone took her hand and pulled her forward to be recognized. It was Kyra, using her small hands to encourage the audience to keep up the applause.

Chloe half raised her hand in a shy salute and quickly stepped back behind the president.

Lucius leaned close and whispered, "I wonder what that was all about."

Beverly just shrugged. She remembered Kevin Stayton, but for the life of her she couldn't remember ever meeting a Chloe Jackson, but she looked great up there and there was no denying that she'd done a fabulous job with tonight's party.

For the most part, Beverly enjoyed the evening. After several glasses of wine, she grew more lethargic and hid more and more yawns behind her hand. Still, she wasn't quite ready to leave just yet.

"Someone is getting sleepy," Lucius whispered as they rocked to Brandy's old jam "Have You Ever?"

"No, no," she lied and then immediately had to stifle another yawn. "Okay. Maybe just a little." She blushed.

"Then what do you say that we head out of here and go do something that will wake you up?" he asked.

Did that mean what she thought it meant? Beverly's legs quivered and those delicious tingles returned. Seeing that she came to the reception with him, it only made sense that they leave together—unless she wanted to play hard to get and call a cab. Looking into Lucius's twinkling hazel gaze, Beverly realized an undeniable truth: she had no desire to play hard to get.

"Yeah," she answered in a lusty voice. "Let's get out of here."

Chapter 5

When Lucius asked Beverly if she was ready to leave, he had meant to extend their evening by going to a nice jazz club or something. But he knew by the look that she'd given him that she had other things on her mind. And he was way too much of a gentleman to disappoint her. As they tried to maneuver through the crowd, Kevin Stayton cut off their escape path.

"Well, I don't believe it! Lucius Gray!" Kevin declared, thrusting out a hand while simultaneously pounding Lucius on the back. "Nice to see you, you old dog."

"Kevin, how are you?" Lucius greeted, though truth be told he'd rather put off their reunion for another time.

"I'm doing good." He glanced around. "You know your old football buddy Terrence is here, too, but you might have some trouble getting to him through his mad fan club."

"So I heard," Lucius said. "Well, if you could excuse—"

"Hey, I've been meaning to talk to you about something. You're a lawyer, right?"

Lucius cast an apologetic look over his shoulder at Beverly.

"Don't worry. I need to step into the ladies' room for a few minutes anyway," Beverly said with a teasing smile. "I won't be too long."

Lucius turned his attention back to Kevin. And though his old friend was delaying his power play, he kept his cool and concentrated on what was being said.

"Yeah, man. The CHRIS Kids Foundation is this great family program that keeps struggling families from collapsing, losing their children and becoming dependent on public welfare, mental health and juvenile justice systems. I was thinking maybe your firm could help them on this. Now, we couldn't pay you much…"

Beverly smiled and waved her way toward the ladies' room, but once inside, her smile dropped and she drew in a deep, exhausted breath. "Bev, do you have any idea what you're doing?" she whispered to herself as she headed over to the long vanity counter to check her appearance. To her great pleasure, her hair was still fierce. Maybe she needed a quick touch-up on her lipstick. She opened her clutch purse and whipped out a pink tube when a weird hacking sound caught her attention.

She frowned. A toilet flushed and a second later, the door opened and an attractive woman in a black sequined cocktail dress stepped out with an awkward smile.

"Are you okay?" Beverly asked, looking at the woman's reflection in the mirror.

The woman looked up and Beverly instantly recognized Tamara Hodges.

"Hey, Beverly. I'm fine," she responded. "At least I will be in a few minutes."

Beverly abandoned her lipstick touch-up and turned to face the pale woman. "Tamara, it's so good to see you again," she stated with a sincere smile. "It's been a while, huh?"

Tamara nodded. "Time goes so fast. You were my first interview for the *Atlanta Daily* after we graduated."

Beverly remembered, nodding. "You did a great job on the article, by the way—I don't know if I ever told you."

Tamara smiled. "You sent me a nice note thanking me. In fact, I believe I still have it."

That was sweet, Beverly thought. Then again, Tamara was always such a sweet girl even though Beverly had always detected a quiet sadness about her.

Suddenly, she stopped smiling. Next she put a hand to her stomach and rushed back into a nearby stall.

Beverly frowned again. "Are you sure you're okay?" she asked a second time when Tamara walked out.

Nodding, Tamara responded, "My stomach is a little upset."

Beverly had other suspicions. "I hope I'm not being too nosy, but are you expecting a baby?"

Tamara nodded sheepishly.

"Congratulations," Beverly proclaimed with bittersweet tears stinging the backs of her eyes. "I—I'm happy for you."

Lucius glanced toward the ladies' room just as Beverly exited. Her smile had disappeared and she looked as though she was downright troubled. "Is something wrong?" he asked when she returned to his side.

"Uh, no. I just ran into an old friend." She glanced over her shoulder, and then smiled back at him. "Are you ready to go?"

Lucius glanced at Kevin and, at last, the brotha seemed to pick up on the hint.

"I'll holler at you sometime next week," Kevin said, winking.

"Thanks, man." Lucius looped an arm around Beverly's waist and this time he managed to successfully escort her from the party. As they strolled out to his car, Beverly leaned her head against his shoulder. Something had changed and Lucius wondered if he'd have to take a rain check for their promised evening.

He whipped out the car keys from his pants pocket, and quickly opened the passenger door. "Here you go, mademoiselle."

"Thank you," she murmured and took her seat.

Once in, Lucius shut her door and then bounded over to the driver's side. Another glance to his right and he knew he had to do something to recapture the moment. "You know those hors d'oeuvres were nice, but I could really go for something to eat. Are you game?"

Beverly pulled out of her reverie and, for a moment, looked like she was going to reject the offer, but then she apparently thought better of it. "Actually, I am a bit famished."

"Great." He started up the car. "Have you ever been to Sambuca?"

A sparkle returned to her eye. "I love that place." She glanced at her watch. "It's dinnertime on a Friday night—do you think we can get in without a reservation?"

Lucius winked. "Leave it to me. I know a guy."

Sambuca, located in the heart of Buckhead, was one of

Lucius's favorite places to dine and dance the night away. On top of offering an eclectic American menu, the casual sophisticated atmosphere was hailed across A-town for the diversity of its live bands. On any given night, its patrons were treated to an evening of jazz, R&B or dance hits.

It was a jazz night, and the low, seductive lighting immediately aided the seductive mood Lucius was aiming for. However, the crowded ring of waiting patrons didn't bode well.

"Yo, Lucius," Spencer, the club's host, greeted the moment he saw Lucius approach the host/hostess stand. "Long time no see. How have you been?"

"Working, you know how it is."

Spencer tossed up his hands. "I hear you, man. Everybody is hustlin'." He glanced over at Beverly and then gave Lucius a knowing wink. "Good to see you, um, testing the waters again."

Lucius caught his not-so-subtle meaning and struggled to keep his grin from turning sly. "How long is the wait?"

Spencer glanced down at the crammed waiting list. "No reservation?"

"Last-minute decision."

Spencer sucked in a long stream of air through his teeth and stroked this thinly trimmed goatee. "I don't know. The walk-ins list is hitting about an hour wait time."

Lucius reached into his pocket and handed over a couple of folded bills. "How about now?"

"Maybe thirty minutes?"

Lucius added a couple of more bills. "And now?"

"Fifteen minutes?"

"You're killing me." He handed over two more Grant

bills, bringing the grand total to three hundred dollars. "My final offer."

"Well, looky here. It appears I *do* have a table in section four available."

"Section one," Lucius corrected, wanting a table closer to the stage.

"That's what I said," Spencer said, grabbing two menus. "Follow me."

Lucius returned his arm around Beverly's waist as he escorted her behind Spencer.

The jazz band jammed John Coltrane's "A Love Supreme" as they moved past the stage and then settled into to their u-shaped leather booths. He and Beverly sat pretty close at the bottom of the *u.*

"Here you go," Spencer said, handing over their menus. "Your waiter should be with you in a moment."

"Thanks, man," Lucius said.

"Heeey—" Spencer shrugged good-naturely "—what are friends for?"

Lucius laughed, thinking about how much his *friend* just bilked him for.

Spencer winked, signaling that everybody had a hustle these days. "Enjoy your evening."

He glanced over at Beverly and loved seeing the huge smile plastered on her face.

She leaned over and spoke into his ear, "I love Coltrane."

Lucius perked at that statement. "Now what do you know about Coltrane?"

"Please. My father was a jazz aficionado. Coltrane was like a god in our house." She laughed, thinking about the number of Saturday mornings she woke to the melodious tune of 'Trane's seemingly magical saxophone.

Lucius nodded appreciatively. "A woman who knows her jazz. You're starting to sound too good to be true."

Beverly couldn't help but blush at the praise and then fell into easy conversation about their favorite jazz artists, which morphed into who were their favorite R&B artists and so on and so on. Throughout the meal, Beverly kept marveling over how easy it was to talk to Lucius. There was something about his smooth baritone that she found comforting. She was convinced that she would be content just listening to him read the phonebook.

When another old favorite began to play, this time "What a Diff'rence a Day Makes," Lucius adeptly read her face and offered her his hand. "May I have this dance?"

Beverly tilted her head. "Yes, you may."

They stood together and waltzed over to the small dance floor before the band. As they'd done for most of the evening and now the night, the two glided into each other's arms, their bodies fitting together perfectly.

Beverly sighed as she leaned her cheek against Lucius and rocked steadily with him. When Lucius started to hum along with the music, she closed her eyes and allowed herself to get lost in the moment. Gone was the baggage of her failed marriage and the stress of running her own business. For the first time in years, she allowed herself to just...*be*.

The music ended. For Beverly it was a little too soon. She and Lucius pulled apart and joined the crowd in applauding the band. When it was time to leave there was reluctance on Beverly's part. She could easily dance in Lucius's arms well into the morning, but as it was nearing midnight, and the dinner club was winding down.

Strolling out to Lucius's parked car, she had to confess, "This has been a long, wonderful evening."

He opened the passenger door and smiled at her. "I was just thinking the same thing—except for the long part. I kinda thought the night flew by."

Their eyes locked and Beverly's body submitted to an overpowering magnetic pull. At the sight of Lucius's head descending, the muscles in her belly quivered and her heart pounded so loud she feared that the whole world could hear it. When their lips finally made contact, Beverly's eyes fluttered closed and, once again, she was lost.

However, this time was different. In her mind, not only could she hear music, but there was also this wonderful floating sensation that made her feel lush and giddy. She pressed closer, greedy for more.

Lucius eagerly gave her what she wanted—what they both wanted. He had spent the evening wondering what she would taste like and he wasn't disappointed. Her lips were amazingly soft and decadently sweet. A man, if he wasn't too careful, could get caught up.

They remained locked together, the kiss growing hungrier by the second. Lucius pressed her body against the car door. Beverly moaned. Maybe their promised evening was still on. To test the waters, Lucius ran a hand up the front of her dress and cupped one of her large breasts, which easily filled his hand. She didn't pull away. In fact, her mouth opened wider, her tongue delved deeper and mated with his mouth in a way that was so erotic his hard-on was ready to break through the seam of his pants.

However, the sounds of heels hitting concrete and distant laughter penetrated their small intimate sphere and brought them back to Earth. Beverly broke the kiss and panted hard against his ear, "Take me back to the hotel."

Lucius nodded and then helped her into her seat, but

when he rushed around to his own door his throbbing cock made it hard for him to think straight, let alone fold into his seat and attempt to drive. But the moment he was behind the wheel, he gave Beverly one look and then sprang across the seat for one more taste of her sweet lips. She received him with as much hunger and passion as she did a few moments ago.

So soft.

So sweet.

So…

Honk!

Lucius and Beverly sprang apart, their hands shooting up as if the entire Atlanta Police Department had suddenly materialized. Instead they discovered, when their heartbeats slowed down a bit, that all that had happened was Lucius's knee—or at least he thought it was his knee—had hit the horn and that there was no one surrounding them.

Beverly laughed, breaking the tension.

Lucius quickly joined in, cooled down and then started the car. He wasn't the most patient of drivers on the road. The urgency to get back to the hotel gave him a lead foot and rendered him color-blind on a few traffic lights. Hell, it *had* been eleven months.

When the Hilton came into view, his heart lightened as if he was once again the college offensive lineman and his team was just a few feet from scoring the game-winning touchdown. That is until blue lights flashed in his rearview mirror.

No. No. No.

Beverly giggled from the passenger seat.

Reluctantly, Lucius pulled over and then was surprised and relieved when the police car whizzed by, clearly intent on a different destination.

"Maybe you should just drive the speed limit," Beverly suggested with a teasing lilt.

"Right." Lucius pulled back onto the road and somehow managed to control his lead foot and his painfully straight hard-on while maintaining his cool. Well, at least he hoped it came off that way. The flip side was that he was coming off like a dog and at any moment he was going to break out and start humping her leg.

Beverly leaned over to turn the CD player back on. Lauryn Hill's mellow rendition of "Killing Me Softly" set the mood. Now that her libido had the chance to slow down, she glanced over at the man sitting beside her. She still had the same assessment she had earlier. *Damn, he's fine.*

But was she really so bold as to sleep with him on the first night? *Hell, yeah!* the small voice in the back of her head shouted. She could actually visualize a little miniature version of herself, complete with a cheerleading outfit, flipping around and shouting, "Give me a *S,* give me an *E,* give me a *X.* What does that spell? *Sex!*"

Lucius pulled into the parking lot of the Hilton hotel and then shot her a smoldering look that had her twitching in her seat. It was decision time, she realized as he stopped in a parking spot and killed the engine. Beverly closed her eyes and wondered if she could really go through with what her body was demanding. As much as she wanted to recapture her long-lost college spirit, she feared that she didn't know how. The trials and tribulations that she'd endured in the past ten years were like shackles to maturity. Taking risks didn't thrill her as it once did, but rather frightened her. It was sad to say, but the last man she'd been with was her ex-husband, David. What if Lucius found her performance in the bedroom…lacking?

It was possible. David had, after all, escaped her bed for the warmth of another's. Slowly but surely Beverly's earlier confidence started to erode and no amount of pom-pom waving from her invisible self could help her.

Lucius opened his car door and then rushed around the luxury SUV to help her out. "Mind if I walk you to your room?"

No woman in this world could look into Lucius's seductive hazel eyes and deny him anything—her included. "I'd like that very much."

Chapter 6

There was something about the way he touched her.

That was the only way Beverly could explain why she was feeling what she was feeling as they stumbled their way into her hotel suite. She dropped her clutch purse on the floor and kicked her shoes off while Lucius peeled out of his shirt, revealing a beautiful, firm milk-chocolate chest with a nice six-pack.

Yum.

Lucius stalked toward her like a panther approaching his prey; his hungry gaze devoured her every curve.

Beverly's body went haywire while her endorphins had her as high as a kite. She gasped when his arm shot out like a python strike, grabbing her and crushing her body up against his. They melded their lips together in the most intoxicating kiss she'd ever experienced. Spellbound, she slid her arms up his hard chest and then curved them around the back of his head, locking him in place so that she could drink her fill of him.

And drink she did, so much so that the removal of her dress was nothing more than a blur. What did crystallize in her mind was when Lucius gracefully and skillfully removed her black lace bra and tossed it across the room. When his large and strong hands cupped and squeezed her full breasts, a mini-orgasm caused her to break their kiss and gasp her pleasure.

Lucius didn't miss a beat and descended his head lower and sucked one of her hard, raisin-sized nipples into his mouth. A bit of flesh scraped across his teeth and a delicious pain set off another mini-orgasm that caused Beverly's knees to buckle.

They fell to the bed. Lucius adeptly rolled her beneath him so that he could continue to squeeze, suck and occasionally bite at her breasts at his heart's content.

Beverly sighed, gasped and squirmed while mentally dancing near the edge of insanity. Just when she was sure that she was about to take that giant leap, his merciless mouth moved to the valley between her breasts and then traveled lower. Her eyes opened slightly and through the mess of her thick lashes, she watched him descend down the middle of her body.

The erotic part was that he was watching her as well. Despite his smoldering hot gaze, Beverly was more transfixed by the sight of his long, glistening pink tongue. When it reached the center of her body and dipped into her belly button, her lace panties grew moist in anticipation for his tongue's next pit stop.

Lucius peeled her panties from her hips and slid them down to reveal the small nest of curls between her legs. He emitted a soft gasp as if he'd just opened a present to find he'd been gifted with something he'd been longing for forever. First, he pressed a kiss against her springing curls and smiled.

Beverly held her breath for so long that her lungs burned and her chest ached, but Lucius was obviously having too much fun, teasing and torturing her. He pressed kisses against first her right thigh, and then her left, which made her open her legs wider and thrust her hips upward.

Instead of responding to what she so clearly and eagerly offered, Lucius continued to press G-rated kisses everywhere but where she wanted. Even when her soft hands combed his head and tried to direct him, he steadfastly refused to succumb to what they both wanted.

Needed.

However, he was determined to wait for the magic word and given her stark impatience, he suspected he was just seconds from hearing it.

"Lucius," she panted. "Please."

Bingo! He smiled. "Anything you want, baby." He slid his tongue through her soft lips and tasted the honey within. "Mmmmmm," he moaned and then dipped in for another taste, this time longer and taking his time twirling his tongue around the base of her pretty pink pearl.

Tears surfaced and leaked from Beverly's eyes as she continued to squirm around, the air now emptying her lungs as she aahed and oohed through his slow feasting. At the feel of her first full orgasm building, she found herself inching her way up the bed as if she wasn't sure she was ready for such an intense impact.

Lucius dogged her every move, following her up the bed

until she hit her head against the headboard. Now she had nowhere to go as the pressure kept building and intensifying. Her mouth slacked open. It was going to be too big—too much, she decided and then tried to push Lucius away. However, that was like trying to move the Rock of Gibraltar. He wasn't having it.

Preparing for the inevitable, Beverly spread out her hands and grabbed large fistfuls of the bed's sheets and held on. "Oh, God" she moaned repeatedly. Her body's temperature climbed until finally she exploded. Her soul splintered into a million little pieces.

For a few precious seconds afterward, Beverly had no idea where she was or how she got there. Her only guess was that she existed somewhere between heaven and Earth. By the time she opened her eyes again, Lucius had yanked off his designer boxers and his hard dick was swinging in the air, like he was gearing up for batting practice.

He possessed a beautiful work of art: thick, long and hands down the biggest she'd personally seen. Her clit throbbed and her breasts ached for what was to come.

Still drifting on a hazy cloud of lust, she reached for him and was pleased with how he felt both hard and soft at the same time. Wanting to return the great pleasure that he'd just given her, Beverly took the head of his cock into her mouth and sucked gently before tracing the smoothness with her tongue.

"Oooh, baby. That feels nice," Lucius cooed, running his fingers through her hair.

Beverly loved the praise and grew bold enough to grab his hard ass with both of her hands, and then drew as much as she could of him into her mouth.

"Damn," he sighed, his knees buckling.

With her mouth full, she looked up at him, wanting to see what ecstasy looked like on his face. What she saw only turned her on more.

She sucked harder. Faster. Deeper.

Lucius pumped his hips—not enough to choke her, but just enough to deepen his pleasure. Mentally, he was trying every trick in the book to prevent himself from coming too soon.

It wasn't easy.

Beverly's wonderful mouth and amazing tongue suckled and caressed him in a way that had his toes curling and his heart hammering against his chest. He couldn't stand it anymore and jumped back, his dick springing free from her mouth so he could retrieve the gold-wrapped condom from his wallet.

When he came back to the bed, Lucius handed Beverly the packet. "Won't you help me out with this?"

Her long fingers took the condom from his hand and she smiled wickedly as she tore open the packet and then slowly unrolled the condom over his thick pole.

"Ah, you're trying to pay a brotha back, huh?"

"I don't know what you're talking about," she lied prettily.

He climbed onto the bed, easing her onto her back. "You don't, huh?"

Automatically, her long silky legs slid up and hooked around his waist. "Not a clue."

"Now why don't I believe you?" he asked, taking his thick cock in hand and then using it to smack her open clit. "Maybe I should punish you for lying to me?" He smacked her clit again.

Beverly squirmed. What did she do? Now he was going to torture her again before giving her what she wanted. How long could she hold out?

"You know I could just keep you open like this until you confess."

She moaned and squirmed.

Lucius ran his dick from the top of her clit down to the crack of her ass and then back up again. "It's too bad because I really wanted to get a piece of this. But since you don't know what I'm talking about…" He shook his head. "I guess I should just go ahead and get dressed and go back home."

"No. Don't. I was just playing," she groaned and then realized that it hadn't taken her long to break and beg.

"You were just playing?" He placed his dick right at the entrance of her sex and watched her try to ease him in. "Are you playing with me now?"

"No," she sighed. "Please." She was going crazy and no longer cared whether he knew it.

Lucius leaned over, kissed her lips. "Please what?"

She kissed him back. "I need you."

With those words, Lucius eased into her with a slow, gentle thrust of his hips. At the same time, Beverly sank her nails into his back and they both ended up hissing with a mixture of pleasure and pain.

Beverly couldn't believe how much of him she was able to take in. At one point, she thought that she was losing her virginity for the second time, but the truth was that Lucius Gray was a very well-endowed brotha indeed. And just when she thought she couldn't take any more, Lucius completed their joining with one determined, savage thrust.

Beverly cried out, but Lucius's loving murmur and then subsequent kisses dried her tears. Then he began to move and a whole new world opened up behind her closed eyelids. Years of stress peeled off of her, leaving her feeling as light as a feather.

Lucius's cock filled every inch of her and more, but she was determined to ride until she passed out, if necessary. What was amazing was how she had at first felt like Lucius was too much, but then she quickly found that she couldn't get enough. In no time their bodies were coated with sweat.

"Damn, baby. Damn," he repeated continuously in her ear. "You feel soooo good."

The bed was jumping, the headboard was banging and Lucius's and Beverly's bodies were slapping together as if they were all part of some erotic percussion section of a big sex band.

A new heat simmered and then roared to life, signaling to Beverly that she was just seconds away from another mind-bending orgasm. She tried to brace herself, which caused her to tighten her vaginal muscles and, thus, drive Lucius insane.

"I'm coming," they said in unison.

Lucius slanted his mouth over hers. A second later they were victims of an orgasm so violent that all they could do was shudder and collapse against each other. Spent. Exhilarated. Satisfied.

As Beverly slowly came back to her senses, she rained tiny kisses along his shoulder and then up the column of his sweaty neck. That was all it took for Lucius to reboot and harden again.

"Looks like you want to play some more," he whispered.

"How could you tell?"

He chuckled. "You're an amazing woman."

"You're not so bad yourself."

Lucius's brows hiked up.

"I mean…you're an amazing *man.*"

He laughed. "That's much better." He pulled back and

mopped at her still-hard nipples, eliciting a soft moan from her. "And you're in luck," he said, pausing. "I want to play some more, too."

Her smile blossomed. "Good. Then let's have some fun."

Chapter 7

Beverly woke up Saturday morning with a smile on her face and feeling like a brand-new woman. She started to stretch and uncurl from her C-shaped position only to bump into her new lover's still sleeping form. Stopping in midstretch, she glanced over her shoulder and was instantly awestruck by the beauty of such handsome masculinity.

A calm settled over her as she soaked in his peaceful profile. Her gaze roamed from his healthy hairline to his groomed brows, long lashes and even his light morning beard. Slowly, she pulled away from her comfortable spoon position so she could turn and run her fingers along the light prickly hairs of his jawline. Her smile widened as she realized that she loved the feel of it. Slowly her fingers wandered to trace a line around his lips.

Beverly gasped when he kissed her fingertips.

Lucius's eyes fluttered open, his own smile sliding into place. "Morning."

"Morning," she sighed, amazed at how her body was already tingling again.

He reached out and pulled her close. "How long have you been up?"

She quivered at the feel of his morning erection pressed against the high part of her thigh. "Not long."

"No?" He nuzzled her neck.

Beverly giggled, now being tortured by his scruffy beard against her face. "Stop. Stop. That tickles."

Of course, that just ensured he would continue until she squealed for mercy. Instead of giving in this time, Beverly reached for a pillow and smacked him soundly on the head.

Lucius looked up, confused, but then was hit again. When he went careening to the side, he reached for his own pillow and then declared war.

Beverly tried to scramble out of bed, but received a few pillow whacks that had her diving under the bedding for cover.

"Oh, no, you don't," Lucius said, grabbing her by the ankles and trying to pull her back out. "You started this."

Beverly grabbed hold of the bottom edge of the bed and held on for dear life.

"Ah. You think you're slick." Lucius laughed, yanking the comforter and top sheets from the bed and leaving her completely exposed.

She released the bed, grabbed a pillow and flipped around almost in the same motion. Her swing caught Lucius off guard, but it wasn't powerful enough to knock him from hovering over her. She, however, took a direct blow to the face. Despite erupting into a new series of giggles, she renewed her efforts to try to get off the bed.

Lucius, once again, dogged her every move, including when she fell over the side and crawled toward the safety of the bathroom.

They were halfway across the floor—Beverly, naked and on her hands and knees, and Lucius, naked and dragging her firm backside back toward him—when the suite's door suddenly opened and a startled gasp drew their attention.

"Oh, I'm so sorry. I'll come back later," A young Latina maid said, covering a trembling hand over her mouth and quickly backtracking and slamming the door shut.

Beverly blinked a few times, trying to process what had just happened. Finally, she glanced back over her shoulder to see a very amused Lucius smirking back at her. That was all it took for them to collapse with laughter.

After a long and playful shower, Lucius called room service and ordered up lunch…since they had missed breakfast by a couple of hours. His next call was to the concierge, where he gave his clothes sizes and requested new clothes to be purchased and charged to his credit card.

When they sat down to eat, both cloaked in thick, white hotel robes, they were equally interested in playing footsies as they were with actually eating their meals. Beverly still couldn't believe how she was behaving. It was if she'd taken some magic pill and she was eighteen again.

As if.

But it was nice to pretend. She also ignored the needling question as to what she expected from all of this. Was she officially in a relationship now or was this some weekend fling to help her find her groove again? She bit into her chicken sandwich and eyeballed her lover from across the small table. How nice would it be to wake up every morning to see his handsome face, smiling, laughing and devouring her with a simple glance?

Stop that! she mentally admonished herself. Hadn't she been down that disastrous road before? Hadn't she convinced herself that she was in love before? Hadn't she tried to achieve having the perfect family before?

Soon, her smile melted from her face as a precious memory bubbled to the surface.

Lucius noticed the change immediately. "Is something wrong?"

Beverly jumped as if suddenly remembering he was still in the room with her. "No. Everything is great." She smiled awkwardly.

Lucius's antennae shot up. He'd been around enough women to know not to buy that line. He reached across the table and caressed her hand. "C'mon. Surely by now I've proven that I'm a pretty good listener."

Beverly drew a deep breath and looked as if she was weighing her answer.

The familiar sound of his BlackBerry ringing caught his ear. He groaned and rolled his eyes. Couldn't he have this one Saturday away from the office? It rang again. "Hold that thought," he told her and then bounded out of the chair and searched through the piles of clothes littered across the room for his phone.

Beverly took the moment to regroup and clear her head. *Get a grip, girl.*

"There you are," Lucius said after finally finding the phone, but not in time to answer it. But when he read who the missed call was from, he took a seat on the edge of the bed and returned the call. "Give me just a second," he told Beverly while he listened to the phone ring over the line.

Beverly returned her attention to her lunch until she heard Lucius say another woman's name.

"Erica," he said. "You just called?"

"Where the hell are you?" Erica snapped. "*Your* daughter wanted to see you today so we swung by your place and you're not there!"

"What do you mean you swung by? You were supposed to be going out of town *again*, don't you remember?"

"Well, we changed our minds and Ruby said that she wanted to see you."

Lucius huffed and glanced at the clock. "Fine. I'll be home in a half hour."

"Naw. Don't do us any favors. You're probably out partying with some bimbo while your daughter is in tears."

Lucius gripped the phone and clenched his teeth. "You're out of line. I said I'll be home in thirty minutes so I'll be there in thirty minutes."

"Then you'll be there by yourself because I'm not driving back across town."

Breathe. "Then I'll come to your house and pick her up."

"Well, we won't be there, either. To make her feel better, Andrew and I decided to take her down to Pine Mountain to see the safari. You know how much she loves animals."

"Then *I'll* take her."

"Next time," Erica said and then disconnected the call.

A seething and incredulous Lucius was left staring at the phone, a long stream of expletives flowing through his mind, but not out of his mouth—though the urge nearly overpowered him.

"Is something wrong?" Beverly asked.

"No. Everything is great." Realizing what he'd just said, he looked up. They smiled. "Why don't we make a deal?" he said, returning to the table. "We leave whatever troubles we have at home." He takes her hand again. "Let's just shut everything out and enjoy this weekend."

Beverly's smile returned. "Now *that* sounds like a wonderful idea."

The Hollington Lions homecoming game was against their decades-old rival the Greenville Rangers. It all had the makings of being a really tight and intense game and Beverly was surprised that she was actually looking forward to it. She and Lucius made the last few minutes of the large tailgate party. Like her, Lucius had no problems reverting back to his college days when he kept running across old football buddies that were determined to show off by tossing a football around.

Lucius went a little overboard. Every time he turned or made a play, he checked and made sure she was watching. It was sort of cute, really.

The party wasn't all fun. Darcy and her posse continued to cross Beverly's path and each time they had their noses turned up and their asses on their shoulders. It just confirmed to Beverly that some people never grew up.

The football game turned out to be a real thrill. Lucius and Beverly joined the crowd in shouting and jeering.

Hollington's marching band jammed, playing an array of hits from the '90s, everything from R. Kelly to TLC, and the crowd loved it. Afterward, the college's president took the stage and welcomed the crowd. Chloe Jackson followed behind him.

"Is everybody having fun yet?" she shouted.

The stadium crowd cheered.

"We're just getting started, and there's so much more to come. Just a reminder that there are several places where you can leave your order forms for official homecoming and class photographs. And there will be someone at the brunch on Sunday to collect them as you're getting ready to leave the campus. Be safe, respect school property and don't forget we need your contributions to the alumni association. Hollington is educating our kids better for tomorrow."

There was another outburst of response from the crowd.

Kevin Stayton stepped forward to talk into the mike. "One more thing before we get out of the way and let the performance begin. I think you all need to know who was the moving force behind this weekend. She doesn't think she deserves any recognition, but how about a Hollington shout-out for *Chloe Jackson!*"

Chloe was pushed forward and her image was immediately enlarged and displayed on the screens erected at both ends of the field. She didn't take the mike again, but merely pivoted to wave at the crowd, who applauded her, as the night before. She smiled and quickly stepped back.

Lucius leaned over. "I'm telling you, there's something up between them two."

Beverly shrugged. "They do sort of make a cute couple."

The rest of the game was a complete blowout. The Hollington Lions won the game 27-11 and Beverly and Lucius exited the stadium, laughing and shouting along with the crowd, *"We're number one! We're number one!"*

They were still in a jubilant mood when Lucius carried Beverly piggyback style back into her hotel suite. She squealed when he tossed her onto the bed and then launched himself on top of her.

"Bev, my dear. Has anyone ever told you that you make one hell of a cheerleader?"

Beverly wrapped her legs around his waist and tugged up his shirt. "Rah, rah, rah."

Lucius held up his arms and allowed for his shirt to be removed. He returned the favor by tugging up her black turtleneck, then planting his face in the valley between her breasts and shaking his head like a rabid dog.

Beverly giggled at his childish antics and didn't protest when his hands then made quick work of unbuttoning and unzipping her designer jeans. She went from being amused to being turned on in a matter of seconds. This time, however, she wanted to take the lead and she playfully rolled Lucius over and helped him remove his own jeans.

"Whoo. Somebody is anxious," he joked, folding his arms behind his head and watching her as she removed his boxers and retrieved a condom from the bag the concierge had delivered earlier.

"You were taking too long," she said, smiling and sliding the condom over his rigid cock. Next, she climbed up and lifted her left leg high over his shoulder, stretching herself wide so she could take all of him when she slid down.

The air left Lucius's body in a long hiss. "Oooh. Damn, baby."

Beverly only smiled and rocked back and forth on his dick like a seesaw.

Lucius grunted and groaned while trying his best not to come too soon, but it was hard. Beverly was driving him wild. Just when he thought that he was losing the battle, Beverly jumped off, flipped around and scooted her booty toward his face while she peeled the condom off and stuffed his hard shaft into her watering mouth.

Loving the instant sixty-nine, Lucius grabbed hold of Beverly's melon-sized ass cheeks, squeezed them and then smacked them a couple of times before parting her open and sliding his tongue so deep he could feel her vaginal muscles tremble. His mouth went to work, smacking and slurping until Beverly's mouth sprang off his dick because she was about to come.

"Ooooh, Gawd," she panted.

Lucius continued even as her cries grew louder.

"Ooooh, Gaaaawwwddd." Beverly's body quaked violently as she came, but Lucius was nowhere near done with her.

"Stand up," he ordered, giving her ass a good smack.

She stood up while he grabbed a new condom.

"Bend over and grab your ankles."

Beverly obeyed without hesitation, but nearly passed out from the pleasure of his long, thick dick sliding into her from behind.

"Damn, baby. You're so wet," he praised and then immediately started pumping his hips. Soon he reached around and grabbed her full breasts, squeezing and pinching her nipples, but then his smooth strokes became like a violent jackhammer.

"Oooh, baby. That's it! That's it!" she screamed as he worked her G-spot. It was amazing how he filled every inch of her. She loved the combination of pleasure and pain she felt each time he pounded into her. "I'm—I'm coming," she panted.

"Then come on, baby. That's what I'm here for."

Her muscles started contracting, causing Lucius to hiss and curse about how good her body felt. It got so good to him that he had to hike one leg up on the edge of the bed so he could sink even deeper into her warm, slick walls.

Beverly was the first to scream out. Behind her closed eyelids a blanket of shooting stars appeared and swirled around her.

Lucius cried out, his thick sausage-like dick springing out from the force of his explosion.

They fell to the bed, sweaty and panting for air. As if it was the most natural thing in the world, they curled up together and promptly fell asleep. When they woke again, they had about an hour to get ready for the reunion dance at Bollitos.

Jumping out of bed, they scrambled around, showering and dressing at a record pace. In the end, Lucius whistled when he saw Beverly twirl around in a short black dress that looked as if it was poured over her thick curves. But it was her legs and thick booty that drew his attention and nearly forced his dick to give a high salute.

"Ready to go?" she asked.

Frankly, he was more interested in getting her out of that dress.

"Later," she said as if reading his mind. "I promise."

"In that case," he said, offering her his arm, "let's go."

Chapter 8

Beverly and Lucius arrived at Bollitos at eight-thirty and the place was packed. When Beverly learned that the building was owned by Kevin Stayton, she was more than a little impressed with the five-story warehouse building. It looked quite urban and stark from the outside, but inside was another story altogether. Large, multilevel balconies looked down on a huge five-story dance floor. There was different music playing on each floor.

When they walked through the large double doors, Beverly handed over her jacket at the coat room and then excused herself to go to the large restroom down the hall.

"I heard she was going to be waving on some float tomorrow." Darcy's snarky voice drifted to Beverly when she cracked open the door.

Kitty barked with laughter. "Like she's still relevant or something."

Natalie chimed in. "Who cares that she was home-coming queen a decade ago? She's no better than any-body else here."

Darcy's high-pitched laugh grated across Beverly's nerves. "Tell me about it. If her ass was all that, she would've been able to keep her husband." Her voice lowered. "I heard David left because she went crazy after losing—"

Beverly pushed open the door and stormed inside. Darcy and her gossiping group swung apart and then smiled up at her.

"Bev," Darcy cooed. "We were just wondering if you were coming tonight."

Beverly glared at the woman, letting her know that she'd heard every word.

"Well—" Darcy smiled tightly "—I guess we better get back out to the party."

Beverly remained mute, staring them down and ready if any of them said something out of pocket again. When they sauntered past her they were careful not to bump into her. Likely, they sensed she was just seconds from yanking out their ratty-ass weaves from their heads.

Once they were gone, Beverly closed her eyes and sucked in a deep breath. It did little to calm her down. In fact, she could feel a wave of tears rushing forward. She couldn't decide what was worse, that Darcy was spread-ing lies about her divorce or that she knew the truth about her loss and her subsequent breakdown. Having her years of chronic depression, medication and therapy being dis-cussed and dissected by those cackling bitches had her blood boiling.

"Damn it, Kyra. Why did I let you talk me into doing

this?" She moved over to the vanity mirror and stared at her reflection. Suddenly, she didn't like anything she saw: her hair, her makeup or her dress. After all, who was she trying to fool—her classmates or herself?

She drew a few more deep breaths, but her solitude was disrupted when more women began to drift into the ladies' room.

"Hey, aren't you Beverly Turner?" a woman asked.

Beverly blinked back her tears and forced on a plastic smile. "Yes."

The woman's smile beamed. "Hey, I'm Shawna Miller. You probably don't remember me. I used to be in your English and calculus class senior year."

"Oh, hi."

"I have to tell you," Shawna went on, "I admired you so much back in college. You were so beautiful—and you still are. Plus, you had that gorgeous boyfriend, David Clark, and you were sooo popular with everyone. It just looked like you had the perfect life. I heard you were going to be in the parade tomorrow?"

Beverly's smile tightened. She needed to get out of there. "Excuse me," she said and then hightailed it out of the bathroom.

Lucius saw the look on Beverly's face when she came out of the bathroom and was instantly concerned. "Sweetie, are you all right?"

She glanced up at him, her eyes glossy.

"That's it. No more bathroom breaks for you. Every time you leave my side you come back looking as if someone kicked your puppy or something."

His joke was rewarded with a small smile. "There. That's better," he praised.

"I need to find Kyra," she said. "There's no way I'm riding in that parade tomorrow."

Lucius frowned. "Why? Is something wrong?"

"I don't want to talk about it. I just need to find Kyra…or Chloe Jackson," she amended, as if remembering the name. "I could tell her."

Lucius looked around. "Well, I haven't seen either one of them. Maybe they're over near the stage. I heard someone mention a few minutes ago that Micah Ross was here and about to introduce one of his artists."

"Then let's go over there," she shouted, taking him by the hand and pulling him along. She seemed like a woman on a mission again. He wondered what had happened in the ladies' room that spooked her from wanting to participate in the parade.

They maneuvered skillfully around black leather sofas and acrylic tables that flanked the dance floor. But when the lights dimmed, it became clear that they weren't going to be able see let alone search for anyone. "Hey, let's look for them after the concert," he suggested when he noted her distraught face. "C'mon. It's gonna be all right," he assured her and then led her toward one of the private balconies while everyone else was focused on crowding onto the dance floor.

Beverly allowed him to direct her away. Once they found an empty private balcony, they took their seats on a plush velvet love seat and stared directly down on the main stage. A minute later, college alumni Micah Ross took to the stage to roaring applause.

Lucius leaned over to Beverly. "I still don't remember this dude from school, do you?"

She shook her head. "But he certainly made out well in the music industry. That's no small feat."

After the crowd calmed down, Micah introduced Justice Kane to the stage. Everyone went wild again. The music was good—damn good, actually—and Lucius ordered them a few drinks, hoping to loosen Beverly back up. For a while it looked as though it was working until she spotted someone down in the crowd.

"Chloe!" She hopped up and took off.

Confused, Lucius set his drink down and went to find out exactly what was going on.

Beverly bumped and shouldered her way through the crowd. With her heart in her throat, she grabbed hold of Chloe's hand. Chloe glanced over her shoulder.

"I've got to talk to you," Beverly said urgently.

"But Kevin wants me…"

"I *really* need to talk to you. It's about tomorrow."

"Chloe!" Kevin Stayton shouted.

"I'm coming. I'll be right there," Chloe said. Then she retraced her steps back to Beverly.

Beverly moved away from the stairs and stood near the quiet corridor that led to the restrooms. There was no traffic for the moment. She gnawed on her lower lip, and shifted back and forth from one heeled foot to the other.

"Are you all right? What's wrong?"

"Chloe, I'm so sorry to do this, but I can't be in the parade tomorrow."

Chloe stared at her, openmouthed. "Wha—what did you say? You're not…"

"I can't. I know I said I'd do it, and I really hate to put you on the spot like this, but I can't."

"But why, Beverly? I mean, you don't even have to do anything. You ride on the float and smile and wave. You don't have to *say* anything."

"I know that, but…I'm afraid I'm going to fall apart. I'll embarrass myself. I can't do it," she said, though it was sort of stretching the truth.

Behind them, Micah Ross took the stage again and talked to the crowd.

"Maybe you could think about it overnight? You can call me in the morning. But please don't say no right now," Chloe pleaded.

Beverly shook her head.

Kevin Stayton now took the mike. Chloe gasped. Her gaze went to the stairwell, and then back to Beverly.

Before Beverly could say anything else, Lucius grabbed her arm and pulled her back.

"What the hell is going on with you? You've been acting strange ever since we got here."

"Nothing. Everything is fine now." She smiled sweetly, feeling as if a load had been lifted from her shoulders.

Lucius frowned at her ability to run hot and then cold within the blink of an eye. "Are you sure?"

"Yeah." She eased past him to head back to their private balcony.

Still frowning, he followed her.

"And here she is!" Kevin proclaimed from the stage.

Beverly and Lucius returned to their love seat and stared down at the stage.

"I am delighted, thrilled, relieved and proud to introduce Chloe Jackson to everyone…"

The crowd went wild with applause.

"…as my future wife."

"Hot damn," Lucius laughed. "I *knew* something was going on with those two."

Chloe took the mike and waited until everyone had

quieted down. "I know you're sick of hearing my name by now. I apologize for Kevin being such a bore about it…."

Someone laughed out loud. More laughter followed. Chloe looked momentarily confused and thrown by the tittering as she talked. "I appreciate Kevin's…his…uh…"

Chloe stopped and blinked. The laughter grew.

Beverly smiled as her eyes misted. "She didn't hear him."

Chloe's eyes widened as she turned toward Kevin. "Did you…what did you say?"

"Awww. This is so sweet," Beverly murmured to herself.

Kevin took the mike back, put his arm around Chloe's waist and pulled her close.

"I said, Chloe Jackson, will you marry me?"

The crowd went wild.

A chant began on one side of the stage. It picked up on the other, and suddenly began a wave around the room.

"Chlo-*e*, Chlo-*e*, Chlo-*e*…"

"Say yeessssss!" a woman yelled. Everyone laughed.

Chloe turned to Kevin. "Yes," she choked out, almost inaudible. "Yes, I will," she said a little louder, nodding.

"Ke-*vin*, Ke-*vin*, Ke-*vin!*"

Chloe reached for the mike and spoke clearly into it. "Yes, I'll marry you, Kevin Stayton."

The room erupted into wild cheers and whistling and applause. Beverly and Lucius jumped to their feet to applaud the couple. Beverly even wiped away a tear, which surprised her. She thought that all her romantic fairy-tale notions were long dead and buried. She personally knew what happened after the glittering ring and the "I dos." *Maybe it will be different for them,* she reasoned. At least she hoped so.

She smiled and watched the couple kiss and spin around on the stage. Yeah, she decided. It *will* be different.

When the newly engaged couple exited stage left, a local Atlanta band, Déjà, took to the stage and launched into a rendition of Notorious B.I.G.'s "Hypnotize." Lucius and Beverly took one look at each other and, like most of the attendees, bum-rushed the dance floor to get their groove on.

Shaking and gyrating bodies monopolized the floor and Lucius was determined to show that he knew how to pull up to her bumper like just like the best of them. Beverly lost herself in the music as it shifted from East Coast driving bass to West Coast's hot beats like Dr. Dre's "The Chronic" and then polished off one set with R. Kelly's remix of "Bump and Grind."

Lucius was so all over her that it looked like he was glued on—and Beverly didn't mind at all. Shortly after that performance, they hurried out of the club just short of midnight. They were so hot for each other that they couldn't keep their hands off each other during the drive back to the hotel.

Beverly abandoned her seat belt so she could kiss and suckle his earlobe, while jamming her hand down in his crotch and stroking her new best friend. "Wait till I get you back to the room," she whispered and then slowly glided her tongue down the shell of his ear.

He shivered and reached a hand in between her legs. He slid her moist panties over and slid a finger deep into her wetness. "Looks like you're already ready for me," he said.

She sighed sexily against his ear and then moaned when a second finger joined the fray. To prove that she could keep up, Beverly unzipped his pants. "I hope you know how to concentrate," she said, then folded over into his lap and took him into her mouth.

Lucius nearly swerved out of his lane. He removed his

hand from her body and then planted them at ten o'clock and two o'clock on his steering wheel. However, the feel of Beverly's warm mouth, coupled with the tightness of squeezing to the back of her throat, caused his toes to curl up off the accelerator to the point that he was driving a good twenty miles below the speed limit.

When Beverly's head began to bob at a faster pace, he could literally feel tears brim in his eyes, while his lungs felt as if they were on the verge of collapsing.

"Ooooh. Sssssssssh," he hissed repeatedly. Thank God the hotel finally came into view. But he had a hard time turning the wheel at the feeling of orgasm brewing at the base of his cock. Somehow he managed not to sideswipe a car that was leaving the hotel lot. Wanting to continue this groove that they were on, Lucius found a parking spot toward the back of the hotel and killed the engine.

Grinning, Beverly lifted her head and asked, "Condom?"

"Wallet. Back pocket," he panted and raised his hips.

She reached around and pulled out his wallet. After ripping the gold packet open and sliding on the condom, Beverly climbed onto his lap.

Lucius did his part by hitting the automatic button to slide his seat back so they could have a little more room to work. He didn't have long to wait as Beverly slid her panties to the side and eased down on him in one smooth motion.

"Aaaaaaahhhh," they both said as their bodies sighed in relief.

He hit another button and his seat reclined all the way to the back so he was practically lying down.

She leaned forward and drew his soft lips into a deep kiss while she began to ride him slowly and deliberately. Listening to his moans and groans filled Beverly with a power she hadn't felt in such a long time that she couldn't help but revel in it.

"You like this, baby?" she asked, squeezing her vaginal muscles.

Lucius sucked air through his gritted teeth and nodded.

"Let me hear you say it," she ordered.

He smiled wickedly, knowing the game they were about to play. "I love the way your body feels, baby. Especially when I do this." He surged his hip forward, rammed himself in all the way to the hilt.

She gasped, feeling like a tiny firecracker shot off toward the tip of her clit.

"Or when I do this." He surged forward twice in quick succession, making a hard smacking sound. To prove that he could take control at anytime, Lucius locked his hands around her waist and held her in place while his hips pounded away.

Beverly could barely breathe, let alone think, and she certainly couldn't be held accountable for whatever nonsense that spilled out of her mouth while Lucius tried to drill his way to China.

As if their bodies were totally in sync, a violent tremor erupted and then surged through both of them like a bolt of lightning. When it passed, they were left hot, sweaty and panting.

"Damn. Has anybody told you that you're amazing?" Lucius asked once he was able to talk again.

"You might have mentioned it." She smiled and peppered his face with kisses.

"All right now. If you keep that up we're going to have to go another round."

"Promise?" She nibbled on the bottom of his lip and then grinned when she felt his cock quicken again.

Lucius gave her a hard smack on her ass. "Let's get you upstairs. There's a few more positions I'd like to try out."

"Good. I have a few of my own."

Chapter 9

The hotel suite was a wreck. Clothes were tossed everywhere, while chairs, desk tables and a nightstand were also overturned. Somehow the king-size mattress had gotten tossed off the box spring so that now half of it was on the floor. Coincidentally, it was the part they had fallen asleep on.

There was a phone ringing somewhere. Beverly half hoped that it was somehow a part of this wonderful dream that she was having where she and Lucius were laughing and playing with this most adorable little girl. The child looked so much like Lucius, with his beautiful brown skin and quarter-size hazel eyes, that Beverly's heart stirred and an old longing returned.

But the damn phone kept ringing.

Beverly opened one eye, looked around and was confused by the utter destruction around her. Had a hurricane hit the hotel? The phone rang again. She lifted her head, looked around. This time, she noted, Lucius snuggled up against her as if he'd fallen asleep suckling her breasts.

She felt around, her hand seeking for the ringing phone. After stretching a bit, she found it up near the wall and yanked up the handset. "Hello?"

"I know Ms. Thang ain't still sleeping?" Clarence said with a sarcastic chuckle. "Why didn't you answer your phone when I called? I know your butt turned in early."

Beverly turned her head back toward Lucius. "Um, not exactly."

Clarence emitted a small gasp. "Don't tell me you actually stayed out at that reunion dance and had a good time."

She giggled. "More like I've been having a *great* weekend."

"Whoooooooooo, Beverly girl!"

Beverly jerked the phone from her ear and then shook her head to stop it from ringing.

"C'mon. Spill it. Spill it," Clarence insisted.

She could actually picture him in his morning pink robe, with his heel propped up in a kitchen chair while sipping his morning coffee.

"Is he fine, girl? I know he's fine. Was it that freakum dress you had on Friday night? I know it was."

"Do you even need me for this conversation?" she asked.

"Hell, yeah," he drawled. "I need details. It's been so long since you got laid, I feared you were walking around with the Sahara Desert between your hips."

"Now you're just trying to be funny."

"And you're stalling."

Lucius stirred and then surprised Beverly when he latched onto one of her breasts like it was the most natural thing in the world to do first thing in the morning. With a few gentle strokes her nipples peaked and hardened.

Beverly closed her eyes and felt other parts of her body start to reawaken.

"Bev, do you hear me, girl?"

"Huh?" she said almost dreamily. Lucius's hands started roaming over her body, forcing her to spread her legs so he could test the wetness within. "Oooh."

"Awwww, hell naw," Clarence squealed. "I *know* that you're not still gettin' your freak on while I'm on the phone!"

"I'll have to call you…b-back," she panted and then slammed the phone down.

Lucius's head descended down her body. "I hope that wasn't important," he rasped, peeling open her legs like her body was a precious flower.

"No. This is more important," she said, guiding his head down and sighing when his mouth dipped inside to taste her body's fresh morning juice. At this point, Lucius knew her body like the back of his hand. He knew just how many licks it would take to make her come or how to tug gently on her clit to prolong the moment.

Right on time her clit started going through convulsions. Beverly closed her eyes as Lucius worked his fingers and his mouth faster and faster while her legs fluttered around his head like an erotic black butterfly.

At long last, she screamed out his name as her body imploded.

"How you feel, baby?" he asked, peppering kisses against her firm thighs.

Was he kidding? She felt amazing.

The suite's door swept open, the lovers jerked their heads to see the same Latina housekeeper from yesterday gasp with shock. "I'll come back later," she said *again* and then quickly backed out of the room.

Lucius looked up at Beverly's cranberry-red face. "I think she does that on purpose."

Beverly covered her face with her hands, embarrassed. "We should have put the Do Not Disturb sign on the door."

He nodded, realizing that was probably a good idea.

The phone rang again. Beverly had a sneaking suspicion that it was Clarence calling her back. She grabbed the phone, ready to have a little fun with her friend. "What is it, bitch?"

"*Excuse* you?"

The unmistakable feminine voice clearly was *not* Clarence. "Who's this?"

"Kyra. Who the hell do you think it is?" she said, offended.

Beverly bolted straight up. "Kyra, I'm sooooo sorry. I thought you were someone else."

"*Obviously.*" She cleared her throat.

Lucius snickered as he climbed onto his feet, his semihard dick swinging in between his legs as he headed toward the bathroom.

Beverly smacked her lips as she watched him.

"Bev!" Kyra shouted. "Are you still there?"

"Huh, what?"

"I was asking you why you're trying to back out on the parade at the last minute? You're about to give my girl Chloe a heart attack. What do you expect her to do at the last minute?"

Beverly was instantly irritated. "I don't know. Ask Darcy Knight to ride on the damn float."

"Is that what all this is about? Bitching Darcy? Forget her. She was a mean, evil girl and now she's a mean, evil woman."

Beverly sighed. "I know, but—"

"But nothing. You're riding that damn float even if I have to hog-tie you to it." Kyra then softened her words. "Besides, you don't want people mistaking Darcy for you, do you?"

Beverly grimaced. "God, no."

"Good. Then it's settled."

It was a statement, but it sounded more like a question.

Beverly knew that it was time to put on her big-girl panties and do the right thing. "All right. All right. I'll do it."

"Great. I'll see you at the brunch."

Disconnecting the call, Beverly stood and wrapped the bed's top sheet around her body. "What time is it?" She glanced around, trying to find the clock among the wreckage. When she finally found it, she saw that once again, she only had one hour to get ready for the school's brunch.

She raced to the bathroom, disappointed to see that Lucius had already climbed into the shower. "You couldn't wait for me?" she asked, dropping the sheet and then stepping in behind him.

"You were on the phone." He turned toward her and started soaping up her body, paying particular attention to some body parts more than others.

Beverly did the same.

When they stopped playing around and got out of the shower, it was clear that they were going to be late.

The brunch was taking place at Hollington's campus on the center lawn, known to students as the quad. There were large tents erected everywhere. It was a huge catered buffet affair with tables of mouthwatering breakfast food and sandwiches.

"I see some pancakes with my name written all over them," Lucius said as he toted their picnic blanket and searched for a good spot on the crowded lawn. There were a lot of children running around, being that the event was geared toward the alumni and their families.

"I wish I could've brought Ruby," Lucius said absently and then sighed.

Beverly had almost forgotten that he said he had a daughter. A surprising stab of jealousy hit her squarely in the heart. It was a strange reaction since she'd only known this man for a few days.

Days.

She shook her head. In some ways, this weekend felt as long as a lifetime and there were parts of her that felt as if she'd known Lucius all her life—that they had always had this amazing connection. A frown teased the corner of her lips. She needed to watch herself. The last thing she needed was to get caught up in something that would never be. She wanted nothing to do with love. This weekend was just about…fun.

"How about over there?" Lucius asked, pointing to a small spot a good hundred paces away.

"Looks good to me."

They quickly settled down and then Lucius took off after taking her brunch order.

"Beverly!"

Beverly turned around and saw Kyra rushing over toward her. She smiled. "Hey."

The women gave each other a brief hug.

"So are we still good?"

Still feeling a bit reluctant, Beverly nodded her head. The best way to get through this day was to just grin and bear it.

"I'm going to have to buy you an ankle bracelet," Terrence Franklin joked, coming up behind her, "because every time I turn around, you're gone!"

Beverly blinked in surprise. What were Kyra and Terrence doing together—again?

Kyra laughed. "Terrence, you remember Beverly Turner, don't you?"

"Of course. You were homecoming queen."

"Congratulations on all of your success, Terrence," she said, smiling.

"Are you enjoying the brunch?" he asked. "It's like one big ol' party out here, huh?"

"You can say that again. Chloe said that brunch would be open to the community, but I wasn't expecting such an enormous turnout."

"This is nothing," he told her. "Wait until the parade. The streets are going to be chock-full with—"

Kyra jabbed in his side. "Beverly's a little nervous about being on the float," she explained, rubbing a hand along Beverly's back.

Nervous? Nerves had nothing to do with it.

"But she has nothing to worry about, right, Terrence?" Kyra asked.

"Just the thought of being on display in front of all these people is making me feel sick," she said, fingering the lace neckline of her cream-colored blouse. "I'm a fashion designer, Kyra, not a beauty contestant."

"You'll be fine." Kyra's voice was bright and full of cheer. "Would it help if we stayed with you until it's time to head over to the stadium?"

"Bev, you have nothing to worry about. It's a fun, family-filled event."

"Kyra's right," he agreed. "You're among friends, Beverly. So, go out there and make the class of '99 proud!"

She gave a low, shaky laugh. "Right, that's easy for you to say. You're not the one on top of that stupid float."

"Bev, you're gorgeous," Kyra told her. "With that pearly white smile and shapely figure, you're a force to be reckoned with, girl!"

"I second that," Lucius's familiar voice said, coming up behind Beverly.

"Hi, Lucius."

He kneeled and set their two plates down on the blanket.

"Well, knock me over with a feather, if it isn't the great Terrence Franklin!" Lucius chuckled. "I've been wanting to talk to you since Friday, but every time I turn around, you've got a crowd of people around you."

"Hey, man, what's up?"

"You don't remember me, do you?" Terrence shook his head. "I figured as much, but I'd hoped that you'd remember the offensive lineman who took all those hits for you in that state championship game."

"Lucius Gray?"

"Attorney at law," he added, with a laugh.

"Man, you were one hell of a tackle. How come you didn't go all the way? With your competitive edge and strength, you could've had your pick of NFL teams."

Lucius pointed a finger at his chin. "I like this face far too much to let it get stomped on every Sunday afternoon!"

Everyone laughed.

"Beverly, can I steal you away for a second?" Lucius asked.

Terrence slipped a hand around Kyra's waist and squeezed affectionately. "We'll see you guys later," he said, nodding at Lucius.

"All right, man, have a good one." Terrence and Kyra strolled off.

Beverly blinked in surprise at the affection being displayed between the couple. Clearly the two had put their past behind them. But what had happened to Kyra's fiancé?

"Bev."

"Hmm?" She turned her attention back to Lucius. "So, what's up?"

"I just wanted to warn you that I ran into—"

"Hello, Beverly."

Beverly stiffened. She knew that voice anywhere. Slowly she turned around to see a face she'd spent the last few years hating—her ex-husband.

David flashed his toothy smile. "What—you're not happy to see me?"

Chapter 10

Lucius was torn.

He wanted to give Beverly her privacy, but there was something about this situation that didn't feel right to him. Not to mention, Lucius didn't like the way Beverly froze the moment her eyes landed on her ex-husband. There was a palpable tension that one needed a chainsaw to cut through. He glanced down at Beverly, waiting to see whether she would give him a signal to leave or not.

Instead, she moved closer to him so he eased an arm around her waist and then leveled a look at David Clark that made it clear that he had her back.

"What do you want, David?" Beverly asked, her voice razor-sharp.

David's smile remained in place. "What makes you think I want something?" he answered as if the question was ridiculous. "Why can't I just come over here to see how my ex-wife was doing?" His gaze finally shifted over to Lucius. "I would've done it last night, but, um, you looked...*a little busy* on the dance floor."

It was Lucius's turn to smile slyly.

Beverly sounded equally unfazed. "Well, in case you haven't noticed I'm still *a little busy.*"

"There you are, baby." Another woman joined the small circle, her arm sliding around David.

Lucius felt Beverly tense even more when her gaze landed on the *very* pregnant woman.

"Oh, hello, Beverly," the woman said.

Instead of answering, Beverly just turned out of Lucius's arms and walked away.

"That went well," David said.

Lucius blinked and then finally took off after Beverly, who had amazingly covered a great distance in a short period of time. When he caught up with her, she kept marching like a solider off to war. He followed while they threaded through men, women and children. It occurred to him that perhaps she didn't have a destination in mind and that she simply just needed to get away.

Needing to break the ice, he said, "You know we're walking away from the food, right?"

"Then go back and eat it if you're so damn hungry."

"Whoa, now." He grabbed her arm and forced her to stop. "Are you angry at me?"

She didn't snatch her arm back, but she did glare down at his offending hold until he released her on his own.

"Look, I'm not...I'm just trying to figure out what's going on."

"Nothing is going on," she snapped.

His brows jumped up. Did she really expect him to

believe that? "So you just storm and stomp around for what...exercise?"

Beverly drew in a deep breath, warring with whether she should even bother to explain. But then she started shaking her head. Why bother? This man was only going to be in her life for what—a few more hours? "Just..." She blinked her eyes dry. "Just forget it. It's a long story and..." She sighed. "I don't feel like dealing with it right now."

One look at his face and she knew that he didn't like that answer. *Well, tough.*

She drew another breath, forced on a smile. "You know what? We made a deal, remember? We're supposed to leave whatever troubles we have at home."

"Neither one of us anticipated trouble following us here."

Beverly cocked her head, indicating to him that she was really trying here.

"All right." He held up his hands. "A deal is a deal." Lucius swung an arm around her shoulders. "So what do you say we get back to our blanket before an army of ants carries away our food?"

Beverly had a decision to make. Let David win and have her run home with her tail tucked between her legs or hold her head up high and enjoy this last day. She glanced back to where she'd left David standing. Him and his *pregnant* wife, Maureen.

Lucius read her mind. "I'm pretty sure they got the message to get lost."

She smiled and said, "You don't know my ex. He can be a little slow on the uptake."

"Then it makes even more sense why it didn't work out between you two." When she laughed, he knew that the day had been salvaged once again. "Come on. Let's go eat before I douse *you* with ketchup."

"Hmm. Now that's something we haven't tried," Beverly said, brightening. Laughing, they crossed back over to their blankets and tried again to enjoy the brunch. A few more old college friends stopped by and everyone reminisced about crazy teachers, crazy couples and crazy parties.

Beverly laughed and cracked jokes but she couldn't help scanning the area for David and Maureen. No matter what tricks she employed, she couldn't stop feeling a lump of injustice in the pit of her stomach. The fact that she'd spent most of her days—years—burying herself in her work, trying to forget, trying to move on, while David clearly had no trouble with it at all.

She pulled herself out of her malaise and flashed a smile whenever she caught Lucius watching her. By now, he probably thought she was emotionally unstable, going from highs to lows within the blink of an eye. Hell, right now she was thinking the same.

It was disappointing and distressing to know her fragile emotions were still so very close to the surface. Perhaps all the work she'd put into herself was for naught and she was no closer to healing than on that first tragic day. Tears rushed forward but she blinked them back and carried on.

The much-hyped parade was to start promptly at two o'clock. Beverly made a quick change into one of her personally designed gold-beaded gowns that she envisioned shimmering and reflecting the afternoon sunlight. Her reunion float was to roll from the college's new stadium, wind around the small local streets and then end at the school's center lawn.

The moment she put on her white sash and checked the

pins holding her crystal tiara in place, Darcy and her cackling crew popped up once again, giving her dirty looks and whispering behind their hands. Beverly had had enough and flipped the women the bird before storming by with her head held high.

As it turned out, the event was a lot more enjoyable than she'd anticipated. The cheers from the crowd as her float glided by performed an amazing job in lifting her spirits. Behind her, Hollington University's award-winning marching band got their jam on and clearly and easily elicited the loudest applause from the crowd.

By four o'clock it was all over and Beverly was pleased to say that she had survived. She stood taking pictures for a while and then changed back into her clothes and caught up with Lucius. He was engaged in an impromptu football game with a few of his old college buddies.

The moment he saw her, he called a time out and rushed to her side. "You looked beautiful up there today," he said, kissing her upturned face. "I was proud of you."

She beamed. "Thanks."

"Are we playing ball or what?" Kevin Stayton yelled.

"I'm coming!" Lucius shouted. Then he asked Beverly, "Do you mind killin' about an hour with these knuckleheads before we head back to the hotel?"

"Sure," she said, and then received another kiss before he raced back off.

"It's almost like watching little kids," Chloe Jackson said, standing next to her.

Beverly hadn't even seen her standing there. "Yeah. I guess." She swallowed a lump in her throat. "About last night and my trying to back out of the parade…"

Chloe waved her off and said sweetly, "Don't worry about it. I'm just glad Kyra got you to change your mind."

Beverly chuckled. "No one can say no to Kyra."

The women laughed.

"By the way," Beverly said, "congratulations. That was a beautiful proposal last night."

Chloe's face darkened with embarrassment. "Thanks. I—I still can't believe it happened."

Smiling, Beverly turned her attention back to the men's game. It was clear to the average observer that the guys weren't as agile as they once were. It took many of them a considerable amount of time to get up once they were sacked. Beverly and Chloe were amused.

At dusk, the game was over, mainly because there were more injuries than touchdowns. Beverly helped a limping and laughing Lucius to his car.

"I don't think a man should be hit that hard after age thirty," he complained. "These bones aren't as strong as they used to be."

She laughed along with him as she tucked herself under his arm and supported most of his weight as they headed toward his car. But as luck would have it, David and his wife were also walking across the parking lot. She tensed, watching David hold open the passenger door of his Mercedes while Maureen struggled to get inside. When he closed the door, David's gaze scanned the lot and he found her staring at him.

He waved and she quickly dropped her head and kept moving.

Back at the hotel, Beverly and Lucius took another hot shower together. But it was all about getting clean instead of exciting each other. They devoured another meal from room service and then promptly fell into a deep, exhausted sleep in each other's arms.

When Lucius woke, the room was dark except for a small strip of moonlight. Yawning, he glanced at the clock and saw that it was well past one in the morning. The weekend was over. He would have to be at work in a few hours. He groaned at the thought of ninety-hour work-weeks, endless negotiations and tedious courtroom battles.

Truth be told, he had a love-hate relationship with his job. He loved being good at it, hated how it usually destroyed his private life. He glanced down at the woman curled in the crook of his arm. Something about the way she clung to him touched his heart.

The question was whether that was a good thing or a bad thing.

Studying her sleeping face, he still saw the naked vulnerability she displayed when her ex-husband came onto the scene. Now, like before, he felt a fierce protectiveness toward her. He didn't know what David had done in their past to hurt her, but he definitely wanted to punch in the guy's face, all the same.

Was *that* a good or a bad thing?

As much as he had enjoyed this weekend, he had no time in his life for a relationship. Hell, he had a hard time trying to juggle weekend visitations with Ruby. Of course, that had more to do with his flaky and unpredictable ex-wife than anything.

We have a deal, he reminded himself. They had this weekend and then they were to walk away. His heart squeezed.

Was *that* a good or a bad thing?

The questions kept coming and he found that he just

didn't have any answers. He liked Beverly—a lot. But now this early Monday morning, he wasn't as sure as he was Friday night that he could have this one wild weekend and walk away, either. Maybe there was some middle ground. Would she be up for that—or was she an all-or-nothing kind of woman?

Beverly stirred in his arms and he automatically pressed a kiss against her forehead. She smiled, though he doubted that she was aware of it. She was so beautiful—but it was clear that there was more to her than what met the eye.

He pressed another kiss to her forehead.

Her nose.

Her lips.

Beverly's eyes fluttered open while she emitted a long kittenlike purr.

Their gazes locked and just like that their passions were reignited. Their light kisses deepened. Seconds later, their hands got into the mix. Roaming and touching and this time stirring emotions that were much stronger than lust. When he entered her, in a weird and erotic sense, it was like sliding into home.

So sweet.

So perfect.

So wonderful.

He started moving his hips; his strokes were slow, deep and languid. Unlike their wild weekend, he wanted to take his time making love to her. He wanted to see how deep he could go, how hard she would quiver and how often she would whisper his name. The intimate moment was heightened by the fact that they refused to break eye contact and it created an invisible bond that shook him to his very core.

Lucius sensed when Beverly's orgasm neared by her

body's small tremors. Suddenly his name was being replaced by small gasps and high-octave sighs. As he
watched her submit to the waves of ecstasy she looked even
more beautiful…angelic.

I could make love to her forever. The rogue thought
drifted across his mind at the precise moment his own
orgasm hit. He cried out her name, shivered and shook
before collapsing and pulling her close.

"Amazing," he panted, feeling a calm settle over him.

Beverly peppered kisses across his chest while he struggled to catch his breath. She was a good woman—a sweet
woman. Lucius definitely wanted to see her again after this
weekend. *Maybe we can work something out in the morning,* he thought as he drifted back off to sleep.

However, when he woke up again, Beverly was long
gone.

Chapter 11

Two weeks later

It was near closing time at Hoops. Beverly felt her patience drawing near an end with a Buckhead socialite who kept griping about the dress Beverly designed to *her* specifications. Of course, it didn't help that every time Ms. Gerald came in for another fitting, ten or fifteen pounds had found its way onto the woman's large frame.

"Are you sure that you let this out?" Ms. Gerald snapped, frowning. "It shouldn't be this tight. If I sit down, it's gonna split straight up the back."

"Yes, ma'am." Beverly rolled her eyes and started removing pins…again.

The bell over the shop's door jingled and Beverly glanced back over her shoulder to see Clarence strolling in wearing a sharp tailored Boateng suit. Just the sight of her friend caused a smile to break across Beverly's face.

"There's my girl," Clarence said, switching his hips toward the back of the store. When his eyes swung to Ms. Gerald, he grimaced. "Now, Alicia, you *know* you need to start pushing back from the dinner table."

Beverly winced and then waited for the inevitable explosion, but to her surprise *Alicia* just smiled while her face reddened with embarrassment. "Maybe I have put on a couple of pounds."

"A couple?" Clarence said, jabbing a hand on his hips. "Giiirrrlll, you better come off that cloud of denial and deal with reality." He walked up to her and pinched her side. "This is definitely more than an inch. Oookaaay?"

Beverly bit and chewed at her bottom lip to keep herself from laughing aloud. Clarence could clearly get away with saying things that she couldn't and she loved him for it. By the time Clarence finished writing Ms. Gerald a reality check, the woman left Hoops with her dress and a vow to call Weight Watchers.

"I swear I should hire you on as a partner," Beverly said, locking the shop's door and flipping a sign to let people know that she was closed.

"Pleeeease. You couldn't afford me." He chuckled and brushed at invisible lint on his suit.

"So why are you so dressed up this evening?" she asked, marching to the back of the store while her evening employees finished cleaning up.

"It's Friday night. You know how I get down. I ain't interested in wasting my weekends with popcorn and Netflix like *someone* I know."

"I'm going to ignore that comment," she said, settling behind her office desk.

"Mmm-hmm." Clarence pushed tape measures, beads and strips of lace out of another chair and sat down. "You should join me tonight. Cassandra Wilson is playing over at Sambuca. You know that place packs in a higher grade of brothers on the regular."

Beverly blocked out everything he said after Sambuca. Instead she was transported back to the night she and Lucius danced cheek to cheek to "What a Diff'rence a Day Makes" and then, of course, what came afterward in her hotel suite. A soft smile touched her lips.

"Please tell me that smile means you'll come?"

She blinked and then frowned. "What?"

"Uh-uh, sister girl. Don't tell me that I'm up in here talking to myself," Clarence snapped.

"I'm sorry," she said, giving him puppy-dog eyes to sell the apology. "I was just thinking about…some business stuff."

"*Business?* Ha!" He made a dramatic show of rolling his eyes. "Now. I guess I have *stupid bitch* stamped across my forehead now, right? You're not sitting there twitching in your seat, twirling your hair and smiling because you're thinking about anything that has to do with business. I know what a sex trance looks like."

"A what?" she barked, trying to sound incredulous but instead sounding guilty as hell.

"Don't play me. You know what a sex trance is." Clarence leaned forward and propped his elbow up on the corner of the desk. "It's that distant look and goofy smile that hits a person's face when they're remembering some good nookie."

Beverly's face burned with embarrassment.

Clarence started snapping his fingers and then pointing at her. "Aha! I knew it! You're still thinking about ol' boy!"

"I am not," she lied and then suddenly got busy shuffling paper around.

"Why you lying?" He laughed. "Ain't no shame in reminiscing, girl. I do it all the time." Clarence waved her off and crossed his legs. "But *then* I pick up the phone and make myself an old-time booty call. If it was good once then it would be good again."

Beverly's body tingled at the suggestion, but she willfully shook her head. "I am not making a booty call."

"And why not? From what you told me, clearly this Lucius guy knows how to tear up a G-spot. You keep telling me that you don't want to be in a serious relationship so why not just have a *special* friend with certain benefits?"

"I thought *you* were my special friend?" she joked.

"If you had a few extra pieces and parts then maybe we could talk," he quipped right back at her. "Until then I think you need to call Luscious Lucius, saddle up and get your rodeo on."

Even though there hadn't been a single day since her school's reunion that she didn't think about her time with Lucius, Beverly stubbornly shook her head. She had made her decision the morning she'd walked out of that hotel room with Lucius still fast asleep. It was harder than she expected, which was the main reason why she had to do it.

Falling in love was not an option. She'd been down that rocky road before and she still had the bruises on her heart to prove it. Who knows, maybe she was like her mother. When she loved, she loved hard—and there was a real dangerous possibility that she could fall in love with Lucius Gray.

"Well, since I'm up here talking to myself again, I'll just go on the prowl by my damn self again tonight," Clarence said, standing.

Beverly blinked out of her reverie again and flashed another apologetic smile. "I'm sorry. I'm just swamped," she said, electing to stick by her *thinking about business* story.

"Yeah, whatever." Clarence leaned down, gave her two quick kisses on each cheek and turned toward the door. "But you know once you blow the top off of that celibacy box it's harder to put it back on."

"Good night, Clarence."

"All right. Act like you don't know what I'm talking about if you want to. You'll see what I mean."

Beverly stared at the door long after he was gone, thinking.

Later that evening, Beverly arrived home. It was the same house she was rewarded in the divorce. She kept telling herself that she was going to sell it, but so far she couldn't bring herself to put it on the market. There were just too many memories—the same ones David ran away from.

She shook her head and entered the cold house. Dropping her keys and purse on the foyer table, she shuffled through the day's mail and then made a face when she saw the Netflix red envelope. "Damn you, Clarence." She tossed the mail on the table and then headed up the stairs.

Every night she tried her best to block out the cold chill, the stillness and the ghosts. Every night she failed. Upstairs, before entering her bedroom, Beverly stopped and then glanced at the room down at the other end of the hall—the same room that had always called out to her. It was the same room that made it impossible for her to ever be able to sell the house.

* * *

"Pancakes! Pancakes!" Ruby cheered, making little bunny hops around the kitchen in her footie pajamas.

"Then pancakes it is." Lucius winked and tugged a chunk of her morning bushy hair.

"And I want lots of syrup," she said, rushing over to the refrigerator.

"It's in the cabinet, baby," he told her as he grabbed all the necessary skillets. "But you can hand me a couple of eggs out of there."

Ruby hopped right to it, loving being her daddy's helper. Together they made big, fluffy golden pancakes smothered in maple syrup. Cooking was a ritual with them since Erica was never really known for her cooking…or cleaning.

However, Lucius was awkward with everything else. His patience was often stretched thin with endless episodes of *SpongeBob* and *iCarly* and his manhood was often challenged when his little princess insisted on his wearing fake pink boas and strawberry-tinted lip gloss.

Despite all that, Lucius was determined to show his little girl a good time. With his visitations becoming more and more erratic he had to make the precious few days that he did get with his daughter special. He was trying his best to make things work without dragging his ex to court. But if things kept going the way they were, he would have no choice but to get a judge to put Erica back in line. Plus, having Ruby over instantly filled his usually cold, lonely house with much-needed warmth and laughter. Not to mention it kept him from obsessively daydreaming about Beverly Turner.

That morning when he'd awoken to find the bed empty and all her belongings gone, he was at first confused and then angry. Sure they had made a previous agreement, but he was offended that Beverly couldn't even be bothered to stick around long enough to say goodbye. In a way, he felt used. The only thing that was missing was money being left on the nightstand.

It didn't stop there.

Thinking about Beverly had affected his work. He was making an unusual amount of mistakes and had almost cost Keith Johnson's widow from obtaining her much-deserved eight-figure settlement. It wasn't like him to be so easily distracted and at times he even wondered why he was so upset anyway. He got *exactly* what he wanted: a wild weekend with no strings attached.

Maybe it wouldn't have been so bad if he had requested at least *one* string. The thought of never seeing Beverly Turner again bothered him. To not hear her laugh, to not see her smile and not feel her incredible body trembling and quaking beneath him—

"Daddy, can we go to the zoo?" Ruby asked, tugging on his arm. "I want to see Yang Yang."

Lucius smiled. Yang Yang was one of the four panda bears at the Atlanta Zoo. Ruby loved pandas—always had.

"Sure, we can go to the zoo this afternoon. I just need to swing by the off—" She frowned and he caught himself. "You know what? Scratch that. No work today."

"Yay!" She bounced around in her chair.

After their late breakfast and a couple more episodes of *SpongeBob,* Lucius got ready for their day trip to the zoo. However, before they could leave, he had to conquer the near-impossible task of doing his daughter's hair. What made it even more difficult was the fact that Ruby was extremely tender-headed. She was whining and flinching long before the brush touched her head.

The end result was always a loose, messy ponytail that had quite a few wayward strands sticking every which way but loose. But she was clean and wearing clothes that matched. In his opinion that put him well ahead of the game.

During the ride out to the zoo, Ruby chatted about everything from her new best friend at school, Penny, to whether or not Papa Andrew was going to buy her a puppy for her birthday. Lucius's hands tightened on the steering wheel at hearing that Erica's fiancé had now been elevated to *Papa Andrew.*

It was the natural progression of things, he supposed, but it was hard for him to think of his daughter calling some other man daddy or *papa.*

"When are you going to get married, Daddy?"

The question was so out of the blue that Lucius was rendered speechless.

"You don't want to get married, Daddy?" she concluded when he hadn't answered her.

"Um. Well…" He cleared his throat. "I haven't really given it any thought, sweetheart."

"How come?"

Another cough. "Well, you know Daddy works a lot and—"

"How come?" She crossed her legs in her seat.

"So I can make a good living and uh, well, so I can support and buy you nice things."

"Oh," Ruby said, sounding disappointed. "I thought it was because you don't have a girlfriend."

Lucius laughed. "Well, there's that, too."

"How come you don't have a girlfriend?"

Another round of sputtering ensued and then he came up with the same answer as before. "Well, you know

Daddy works a lot…and there's little time for, uh, Daddy to find a girlfriend."

Ruby's face twisted in a confused frown. "Papa Andrew works and he says that he's going to marry Momma."

Lucius's hands tightened on the steering wheel again. Now his daughter was comparing him to another man. This definitely wasn't good.

"Don't you get lonely, Daddy?"

He glanced at her, surprised. Were her questions based on curiosity or observation? After staring into her large hazel eyes, his heart tugged at her open and honest concern. "Daddy is never lonely when you're around," he assured her.

Her instant smile warmed his heart…until she said, "I still think you need a girlfriend."

"You do, do you?" He laughed.

"Yep. That way you *and* Mommy can get married."

"To different people," he clarified.

Ruby nodded. "That way neither one of you will be lonely—when I'm not around."

Lucius shook his head. "You're something else."

"I know!" She busted out into giggles. After Lucius found a parking spot at the zoo, they unbuckled their seat belts and started to scramble out of their seats. "What's this?"

Lucius glanced over to see his daughter holding up a shimmering gold earring. Beverly's earring. A half smile sloped across his face as he held out his hand and Ruby plopped the gold jewel into his hand. "This…is an opportunity."

Chapter 12

Wednesdays were normally slow days at Hoops and it was then that Beverly and her employees would perform inventory calculations, rearrange the floor and/or do some intense cleaning. Basically, it was just busywork. Clarence, whose hair salon was just a few doors down, dipped into the shop around lunchtime, carrying two plastic containers of his and Beverly's favorite grilled salmon salad from Le Chez restaurant.

"I'm here to rescue you," he announced when he entered her office.

Beverly looked up from her endless amount of paperwork and smiled. "You're a lifesaver."

"That's what they all say." Clarence fluttered his long lashes and then set their food down on the corner of the desk while he removed his jacket. "You just make sure that you buy me a fabulous gift for Christmas next month. I got my eye on this *gorgeous* Louis Vuitton Bastille bag."

Beverly laughed. "Louis Vuitton? Girl, you better get your man to hook you up. I was thinking along the lines of a free manny and peddy."

"Hmmph. Cheap heifer."

"Whatever." She cleaned a spot on her desk and then reached for her salad.

"I come not only bearing good food, I got some gossip, girl." He pulled out a magazine. "Word is music mogul Micah Ross is getting hitched."

"Really?" Beverly said. "You know he came to my class reunion a couple of weeks ago?"

"I know. I'm still mad that you didn't get me an autograph—at least from that fine-ass Justice Kane."

"You're always mad." Beverly looked around. "What—nothing to drink?"

Clarence's gaze raked her up and down. "Oh, no you didn't."

Beverly turned toward the small personal refrigerator and pulled out two iced tea bottles. "Look at that. Bam! I got you," she said, laughing.

"Good thing or we would've just had to bust out some water up in here."

Beverly took the first bite of her food and moaned her approval.

"If you moan like that over some food then I just know how you—"

"Cut it out," she warned with a sharp look.

Clarence snickered. "Fine. I was just saying."

"So who is Micah Ross marrying?"

"Some writer chick…Tamara Hodges, I think."

Beverly dropped her fork. "Get out of here. Are you for real?"

Clarence frowned at her reaction. "What? You know her?"

Beverly nodded while recalling the brief conversation she had with Tamara at Cork's ladies' room and, more importantly, her admitting her pregnancy. It wasn't hard to draw a conclusion. "Wow. Micah and Tamara." She shook her head. "Seems like a lot of people were hooking up at the reunion."

"Oh? Maybe at your twentieth they'll just cut to the chase and call it an orgy party."

"My goodness. Don't you ever quit?"

"Well, one of us got to be scandalous. It's how we keep balance in the world."

At the knock on her door, Beverly glanced up to Leslie, one of her part-time employees.

"There's someone here asking for you."

She frowned. "Who is it?"

Leslie shrugged and walked away.

Beverly glanced over at Clarence.

"Good help is hard to find," Clarence joked.

She shook her head, took another bite of her salad and then went to go talk to a customer. However, the moment she walked into the front of the store, her eyes instantly zoomed in on Lucius, who was standing in the center of Hoops and scanning through a rack of clothes.

Beverly stopped short and blinked, as if it would somehow erase what had to be a mirage—that is, until Lucius turned and smiled at her. "Lucius."

"Well, I'm glad that you still remember my name."

Leslie and the other employees started shifting curious glances their way.

"What are you doing here?" she whispered, looking around and growing uncomfortable about what everyone might hear.

Unfazed by her less than enthusiastic response, Lucius strolled over to her with his sly grin firmly in place. "What if I told you that I missed you? Would that be so bad?"

She stepped back. "This is not a good time—or place."

Lucius looked around, caught the curious stares and then nodded as if he understood. "Well, what would be a good time—and place?"

Clarence rounded the corner from the back room. "Well, I guess I better get…" He stopped and with one glance at Beverly and Lucius knew something was up.

"Hello," Lucius said, flashing his breathtaking smile.

"Weeelll, heeelllooo." Clarence sashayed his way to Beverly's side. "Now who do we have here?"

An image of two trains colliding flashed behind Beverly's closed eyelids.

When it was clear that she wasn't about to make the introductions, Lucius thrust out a hand to Clarence. "Hello, I'm Lucius Gray. I'm an old college friend of Beverly's."

"Lucius?" Clarence's perfectly groomed brows jumped, and then his eyes slowly drank in Lucius's profile while his own sly smile slid across his face. "Well, nice to meet you. I heard sooooo much about you."

Beverly groaned and wondered if it was too much to ask for someone to shoot her.

"Oh, really?" Lucius's gaze swung to Beverly, who didn't doubt that she was at least fifteen different shades of red. "I guess I should be flattered."

"Mmm-hmm," Clarence said, still checking him out. "And I'm jealous."

"Clarence!" Beverly snapped, finally finding her tongue again.

"What? I'm just telling the truth."

"Isn't it about time for you to go back to work?" she hissed, glaring at him.

"Actually, I…um, promised Leslie I'd help her clean up behind the counter," he lied and turned toward the counter, which wasn't far enough away, so he could eavesdrop.

"So you told him about me?" Lucius said.

Beverly turned back to Lucius, wanting to get him out of the shop fast. "Look, this *really* isn't a good time."

"Maybe *I'm* the one that needs to be embarrassed," he said, ignoring her protest. "After all, I thought what we shared was supposed to be private. You know, just between me and you."

She actually felt a prick of guilt.

Lucius leaned forward and whispered, "It's okay. I forgive you." When he stepped back, he winked.

Feeling as if she was just involved in some type of rope-a-dope, Beverly shook her head to clear her mind and then grabbed him by the arm and pulled him toward the door. "Thanks for stopping by to forgive me, but…"

Lucius didn't budge. In fact, he seemed content to remain standing right where he was. "I haven't said why I stopped by," he said, seemingly amused by her flustered state.

She pulled him again, but he still didn't move.

"I wanted to return something to you."

Beverly stopped, her eyes narrowed with mistrust. "Return what?" She swore to herself that if he whipped out a pair of panties or something she would go ballistic. She watched him carefully as he reached inside his pocket and…produced an earring.

"I found it in the car when I gave you a *ride* that Saturday night."

Clarence snickered and then coughed like he was choking on a gigantic chicken bone.

Beverly was now twenty different shades of red as she snatched the earring from his hand. "Thanks. *Now* will you go?"

Lucius realized that this whole thing was going terribly wrong and he needed to change up his approach or risk walking out of there and never seeing Beverly again. "Maybe we should start over," he suggested. "I get the impression that I've upset you."

Beverly crossed her arms and glared at him. "Now why on earth would you get that impression?"

Clarence popped up like a jack-in-a-box. "Don't mind her. She always acts like an old fuddy-duddy."

"Clarence!"

"Sorry," Clarence said, though he didn't look the slightest bit sorry as he slinked back toward the counter.

Beverly turned back toward Lucius. "We had a deal, remember?"

Lucius shrugged. "Deals can always be renegotiated." He slid his hands into his pants pockets and rocked on his heels. He was taking a big chance laying it all out like this. "I'd like to come back to the table."

She was shaking her head before he was finished talking. "I—I can't," she whispered. "I'm not ready to dive into any kind of relationship right now." Beverly glanced around, hoping she was talking low enough. "Please go."

He considered her words, and then stepped closer to her. "It doesn't have to be a traditional relationship," he whispered. "We can just continue on the same course that we were on. Sex with no strings attached."

Beverly blinked.

Hopeful since she didn't immediately reject the idea, Lucius moved even closer so that their bodies brushed lightly against one another. "I don't know about you but I haven't been able to forget about that weekend."

The mistrust in her eyes vanished and was replaced with remembrance and longing.

"You can't tell me that you haven't been thinking about it, too." He leaned down and whispered into her ear, "Surely, you remember how good we are together. I remember how deep and tight your body felt, and how much you quiver when you're about to come."

She closed her eyes as he continued.

"It's like tiny little earthquakes while you tighten around me, literally causing my toes to curl and my lungs to collapse as I struggle to breathe in your scent." For emphasis, he took a deep sniff of her floral-scented hair. "Say you'll go out with me again. I promise you, you won't regret it."

Beverly quivered as if experiencing a phantom orgasm just from the memory of their coupling. When she opened her eyes, she was staring into Lucius's hazel eyes, which were glazed with passion.

"Say yes," he whispered.

"I—I—"

"Say yes," Lucius insisted gently.

"I—I—"

"Yes!" Clarence shouted.

Beverly jumped and then sprang away from Lucius. How in the hell had she forgotten where she was?

Clarence rushed back to her side and took over the conversation. "Yes. She'll go out with you. What day is good for you?"

Lucius blinked. "Well, um, how about this Friday night?"

"She'll be there."

"Clarence!"

"Shut up, girl. You don't know what's good for you," he said, waving her off. "What time?" he asked Lucius.

"Uh—how about seven o'clock?"

Beverly tried to jump back in. "The store doesn't close until—"

"She'll be ready," Clarence said, wheeling and dealing. "Do you have her address?"

Lucius frowned. "Actually, no."

"Leslie," Clarence called.

Leslie popped up next to them and handed him a scrap of paper.

"She'll be ready promptly at seven o'clock. Don't be late," Clarence said.

"Clarence—"

"Don't pay her any mind," he insisted to Lucius. "I'll have her dressed, ready and possibly tied to a chair. Just leave the details to me."

"And me," Leslie chimed in.

"What is this—mutiny?" Beverly asked.

"Yes!" Clarence and the rest of her employees shouted.

Astonished, Beverly stood there with her mouth opened.

Amusement lit Lucius's eyes. "Seven o'clock it is."

But Clarence wasn't through. "Make sure you bring flowers, champagne and condoms."

"Clarence!" Beverly shouted, stomping on his foot.

"Ouch!" He hopped away from her. "All right. All right. Forget the *flowers*."

Laughing and stuffing her address into his pocket, Lucius finally turned toward the door. "See you Friday night."

Chapter 13

"I can't believe I let you two talk me into this," Beverly whined as she watched Clarence rummage through her walk-in closet for what seemed like the millionth time. He was in search for the perfect outfit for her date.

"I don't see what the big damn deal it," Clarence said, holding up another dress for Leslie's inspection. "It's not like you had anything to do."

Perched on one corner of Beverly's bed, Leslie chimed in, "I think I like that one the best."

Clarence's face lit up over the periwinkle blue one-shoulder gown. "I like this, too. She could rock it with a nice pair of silver hoops and those black pumps we saw a few minutes ago."

Leslie bounced and clapped her hands. "She'll need a little bling around her neck, too."

"See, girl. I like the way you think." Clarence winked.

Beverly rolled her eyes. "Does anybody care what I think—or want?" she complained.

"No!" Clarence and Leslie shouted.

Beverly flinched, astonished by their unrelenting bossiness.

"Besides," Clarence said, laying the dress out on the bed, "I highly doubt that you even know what you want—other than to be left alone in this gilded suburban prison that you cherish so much."

"Ouch." Beverly frowned from the sting of his words.

"Sorry, baby, but the truth hurts. The sooner you face it, the faster you can heal."

Instead of responding, Beverly sat on the edge of her bed and continued to pout with her bottom lip poked out.

Leslie took pity on her and went to her side. "Really. What's the big deal?" She shrugged. "He said there would be no strings attached."

"That's what he said the last time and yet he just pops up out the blue. Looks like a big, *long* string to me."

Leslie persisted. "He told you—to return your earring."

Beverly placed a hand against the young girl's cheek while she shook her head. "You poor, poor naive little girl."

"If you're so scared about strings, then don't whip it on him so hard," Clarence reasoned. "Girl, you need to stop treating men like they have the bubonic plague."

"I don't treat them like that. I treat them like they have the *cheating* plague. Men aren't designed to be faithful—especially when things get tough. I learned that the hard way."

Clarence wasn't falling for it. "Girl, will you exhale already?" he asked, rolling his eyes. "I'm a man and I refuse to believe that nonsense."

"Me, too," Leslie said, frowning. "I believe that there is someone for everybody out there."

Beverly looked at the girl as if she had just dropped from the sky. "How old are you again?"

"Leave her alone." Clarence pulled Leslie to his side. "Ain't nobody talking about you two being faithful. This isn't that kind of relationship. Lucius made that perfectly clear. We are talking fucking...screwing...getting your groove on. Whatever the hell you want to call it. You can't tell me that the last time you two bumped uglies that you didn't come back to work mellow as hell. Damn, we couldn't get you stop singing around the store." He looked at Leslie. "What the hell was the name of that song she was singing?"

"'I'm Every Woman,'" Leslie answered, smirking.

"Uh-huh." Clarence bobbed his head, grinning. "Came back looking and acting all brand-new. Now you've gone back to being a tense sourpuss."

"Am not." Beverly folded her arms and pushed her bottom lip out farther.

Clarence finally relented and went to sit next to her on the edge of the bed. "Look, all we're saying is that you need to look at this as every once in a while you need a little...*tune-up* to keep you in a good mood. And who better to do that with than that gorgeous hazel-eyed hunk? Girl, you were holding out on me. You didn't tell me that he was *that* fine. Don't think I didn't check out the dick imprint in those pants the other day. Mr. Lawyer Man is working with some serious equipment. Oookaaay?" He held up his hand and Leslie delivered a high five.

"Boy, you're a fool," Beverly said.

"No, girl. You're a fool if you don't stop looking a gift

horse in the mouth. Now hop in the shower and wash your hair so I can blow you out, real quick."

With a final pout, Beverly stood and then shuffled her way toward the bathroom. Once she was in the shower, she faced her own insecurities about tonight. The real reason she was nervous about seeing Lucius again was that she didn't trust herself. She had just *barely* managed to walk away from him three weeks ago. The emotions that he so easily accessed scared the hell out her. Lucius was the kind of man any woman could fall in love with—herself included. It was really that simple and that scary. What if the next time she couldn't walk away? Would love and all its thorns scar up what was left of her heart?

The last time Lucius had been this nervous for a date, he had to think all the way back to his junior prom. That night he was convinced that he was going to throw up all over his sixteen-year-old date, mainly because her father was like the police chief of the Atlanta Police Department and he'd not only threatened to kill Lucius if anything happened—harmful or sexual—to his daughter, but he also promised that no one would ever find his body.

There was a lot of pressure riding on this date with Beverly. Mainly because it had been harder than he anticipated to convince her to go out with him again. Actually, he didn't convince her—her friends brokered the deal. If things went wrong tonight he had every reason to believe that she would kick him to the curb again and the door of possibilities would close forever.

It wasn't hard for him to put two and two together and conclude that Beverly's hesitance about dating had everything to do with her ex-husband, David Clark. Lucius would never forget how shaken up Beverly had been when David popped up at the reunion's Sunday brunch. There was a wound there still in need of healing. The crazy part was that lately he'd been thinking about him being the one to heal it. The train on which his thoughts were traveling was headed straight to the town of hypocrisy. What the hell did he know about healing old wounds? He had an ex-wife who couldn't stand him and a daughter she frequently used to emotionally blackmail him. The only way he dealt with his own issues was to bury himself in work.

Like Beverly did.

He frowned. Truth of the matter was that they had more in common than he thought.

Following the directions that were displayed on his GPS unit, Lucius turned on the long spiraling driveway leading to Beverly's house. "Nice," he said, as the stunning two-story brick home came into view.

Coming down the same driveway, Lucius rolled past a black Buick LaCrosse that suddenly blew its horn. He glanced over and saw Clarence and Leslie waving.

"Have a good time! Don't do anything I wouldn't do!" Clarence hollered and then sped past him.

Lucius laughed and shook his head. "Maybe I should put those two on my Christmas list."

However, when he climbed out of the car, there was no mistaking the eerie sadness that permeated the air. *Can a house be sad?* He shook his head, dismissing the crazy thought. He rang the doorbell and while he waited for Beverly to answer, again he glanced around the house and shivered when a strong gust of wind blew and caused a slew of fall leaves to stir and dance.

He heard footsteps approach and then a second later, the

front door pulled open and revealed a different but even more stunning Beverly, compared to just a few days ago. "Wow."

She smiled. "That was just the reaction I was aiming for," she admitted.

Lucius's smile widened. "You changed your hair."

Beverly patted one side of her now-shoulder-length hair. "I just changed it back to its original color. You like it?"

"I love it," he said, staring at her golden locks. They matched her eyes perfectly.

As usual she wore a knockout dress that hugged her thick and dangerous curves. Lucius's erection started to tent his pants. Belatedly, he remembered the gifts in his hands. "Oh." He held up a bright bouquet of yellow roses and yellow Peruvian lilies. "I hope you like them."

Beverly beamed and took a good whiff of their fragrant scent. "Yellow for friendship."

Lucius tapped the side of his temples to indicate how much of a thinking man he was. "And—" he lifted the bottle in his other hand "—champagne."

Beverly's eyebrows arched with amusement. "Does that mean that I don't have to guess what's in your back pocket?"

"Well," he said, grinning, "an old Boy Scout always comes prepared."

She shook her head and then stepped back so that he could enter. "Come on in."

He crossed the threshold and stepped into a yawning stillness that felt a lot like a graveyard. Determined to put on his best face, he glanced around the immaculate and beautifully decorated home and said, "Nice place you have."

"Thanks. Come on in." She led him to the living room and gestured toward a full-length leather couch. "I'll be right back."

Lucius nodded and sat down, still taking in the place. The moment Beverly left him alone in the living room, he was uncomfortable about the house's silence. At his place, at least there were the annoying crickets chirping out in the yard. Here, there was nothing.

It was odd.

He continued looking around. The place was spotless and something told him that the room hadn't been used in a long time. He didn't know how he knew that, he just did. Plus—something was missing.

Lucius stood from the couch and slowly walked around the room. There were plenty of nice knickknacks, an impressive mirror over the fireplace and an interesting silver art-deco clock on one wall and...

Then it hit him. The room lacked warmth, a sense of identity and character because there were no *pictures*. Women usually loved pictures and yet there wasn't a single frame on the fireplace mantel, tabletop or wall.

Beverly suddenly reappeared with the flowers in a vase. "Here we go. I'll just set these down over here," she said, placing them on the glass coffee table. "There, that looks nice."

"Beautiful," Lucius agreed, halfheartedly. He was ready to leave. "I guess we better get going. We have reservations."

"Oh. Okay." She smiled and they both walked back to the foyer, where she retrieved a light black dress coat. "Where are we going?" she asked.

"How about we let that be a surprise?" He helped her slip into her coat and then escorted her out to his vehicle.

Beverly didn't doubt for a moment that Lucius had booked them at some fabulous restaurant for dinner. And he did: Nicholas, a stunning five-star restaurant that was a fixture on the Buckhead dining scene. However, instead of being escorted to a table inside of the restaurant, their host led them to a private table on the roof.

Beverly gasped at the stunning sight of the simple white linen tablecloth and an elaborate display of string white lights and candles. There was even a speaker where the music from the restaurant was being directed up there as well. "I don't believe it." She turned to him. "How?"

"Let's just say that I pulled a few strings." He winked and then led her to the table.

As Beverly walked, she felt as if somehow she was standing on top of the world. Below them was a mass of blinking lights, while above them hung a crystal-clear full moon. "This is so beautiful," she sighed. The little girl inside her felt like spinning around in a circle like a fairytale princess in a Disney movie.

"I'm glad that you like it." Lucius beamed from ear-to-ear.

"I *love* it."

"Madam." The waiter handed her and Lucius menus and then quickly told them about the night's special while simultaneously opening the bottle of champagne that Lucius had brought along. Once he took their orders, he bowed deeply and disappeared back downstairs.

"Okay," Beverly said, "I have to admit that I'm very impressed."

"I do aim to impress and *please,*" he said.

"I can vouch that you can do both very well." She locked eyes with him and took a deep sip of her champagne. Beverly watched as his chest expanded with pride.

"You better watch out. You're gonna make a brother start blushing."

"Now that I would like to see."

His brows jumped. "Shall I tell you what *I* would like to see this evening as well?"

It was Beverly's turn to blush. "I think I might know what that might be," she said. "Who knows? Maybe if you play your cards right, you might just get what you want."

"Then expect me to be a good boy all night."

She exaggerated a frown. "I don't want a good boy."

Lust suddenly polished Lucius's hazel eyes. "Don't play with me. I'll have you spread out on this table in a hot minute."

"Promises, promises, promises," she teased just as the waiter and two servers waltzed out onto the roof, carrying their food.

Their eyes remained locked together as their plates were set before them. Their bodies were warming at the thought of what the night held for them.

"Will there be anything else?" the server asked.

"Yeah." Lucius pulled out a folded hundred-dollar bill. "We'd like to be alone for the rest of the night. If we need anything else, we'll call downstairs."

"Yes, sir." The waiter accepted the tip with a gracious smile and then gave them another deep bow before ushering the other servers back downstairs.

Beverly held her laughter in check until they were alone again. "Now you've given them the wrong impression. Lord only knows what he thinks we'll be doing up here."

"Whatever he's thinking I hope he's right," Lucius said.

"What—up here? I was joking earlier."

"I wasn't."

Beverly blushed again and took in her dreamlike surroundings.

"Have you ever made love outside before?"

"You *know* I have."

He waved that admission off. "A car doesn't count since technically you're inside of something."

"I'd like to have seen you tell that to a cop had we been caught."

"You're avoiding the question," he countered, smiling.

"I never really thought about it," she said, stalling.

Lucius chuckled. "So think about it now."

"Okay…so…maybe I haven't." She shrugged.

"Ahh. So I could be your first."

"I guess that's one way of looking at it."

Lucius wiggled his brows. "I will."

They continued to give each other teasing looks while they ate their meals. Though the food was wonderful, it was hard for Beverly to concentrate on anything other than the possibility of making love to Lucius on the rooftop.

"What's the matter? Are you not hungry?" he asked after noting the small bites she was taking and how much food was left on her plate while his was almost clean. "If you don't finish your meal, you won't be able to have your dessert."

"Dessert?" Her heart started pounding.

"Mmm-hmm." He nodded. "Dessert is the best part of the meal. My favorite is something chocolate…with a creamy center."

Beverly twitched in her seat.

"Don't you like chocolate?" he pressed.

Beverly thought the altitude must be affecting her brain because suddenly she could barely think, but after a long pregnant silence she managed to whisper, "I love chocolate."

Lucius grinned. "That's what I remembered."

She grabbed her glass and tossed the champagne down her throat like it was water. This brother had all kinds of memories playing in her head. When she looked back over at him, she couldn't seem to get her gaze to rise above his luscious smile. The man had the sexiest pair of lips she had ever seen. Every few seconds she caught his pink tongue darting and gliding across his lips, and could feel her panties dampen a bit. Good Lord, how on earth had she been able to make it three whole weeks without that mouth caressing or kissing her body?

A new song began to play over the speaker and Beverly instantly recognized the first few bars of "What a Diff'rence a Day Makes."

Lucius recognized the music as well. "Would you care to dance?"

She smiled. "I would love to."

He stood from his chair and walked around to assist her up. Standing from their table, Lucius took Beverly into his arms and they swayed together cheek to cheek. As before, Lucius hummed in tune to the music and Beverly's mind wandered.

How was it that being in his arms melted away all the stress and challenges in her life? If she allowed herself to be truthful with herself she felt completely and utterly safe in his arms. Nothing and no one could harm her while she was with him. Beverly closed her eyes and hummed along with him. She liked the way their voices blended together.

"Maybe we should take this act on the road," Lucius whispered in her ear.

"Celebrity couples rarely make it." Her eyes fluttered open when she realized what she had said.

Lucius pulled back so that he could stare directly into her face.

Beverly saw that there was a question in his eyes and for a few heart-pounding seconds she was afraid that he'd give voice to it. Instead, he smiled, kissed the tip of her nose and clearly decided to let it go. She placed her head back against his cheek and mentally said a prayer of gratitude because…what was she thinking? Was she secretly wishing for more than what he offered—more than she confessed to wanting?

Seconds later, she felt his soft lips pressing against the shell of her ear, then her cheek, and before she knew it they were sharing a gentle but soul-stirring kiss where their tongues danced and caressed one another. *Oh, God, he tastes so good.*

Lucius's hand crept down her back and then suggestively slid across and around her thick booty.

Beverly pushed herself up against his firm frame and gasped when she felt his bulging erection press back against her pelvis. Without thinking she reached down, cupped him and then started stroking through the seams of his pants.

Lucius sucked in a long breath through his gritted teeth. "You know you shouldn't be starting anything you can't finish, right?"

"What? I thought your little friend just wanted to say hi to me."

"Little?"

She laughed at his inflated ego. "Hmm. Maybe I need some help with my memory."

"Maybe." He kissed her again, sucked on her bottom lip. "Come over here." He directed her back to the table and sat down in his chair. "Have a seat." He patted his lap.

Beverly hesitated.

"What—you scared?" he asked.

"Of course not," she said, accepting his challenge and taking a seat on his lap.

Lucius smiled and tipped her head toward him so he

could reclaim her lips, but while he did so his free hand cupped and squeezed her breast.

Maybe it was the music, the night's air or even the full moon that emboldened Beverly, but she went back to cupping and stroking Lucius through his pants. As her hormones continued to spin and her body started to heat, she took it a step further by unzipping him and then caressing him through his black briefs.

"Don't stop there," he whispered.

Should she dare—out here in the open?

He pulled back from her lips to stare up into her eyes. "You don't have to if you don't want to."

At that moment, more than anything she wanted to please him *and* she wanted to do something that she had never done before. Summoning her courage, Beverly freed his erection from his briefs and exposed him to the sultry night air. She smiled, loving the feeling of holding him like this again.

Lucius moaned, "You have *wonderful* hands."

The praise only stroked her ego. "You like that, do you?"

He nodded. "You know what I'd like better?"

She waited.

"Stand up," he ordered.

Beverly did as she was told.

Lucius took a good long look at her. "I love that dress on you," he whispered, reaching out and slowly lifting it up. "It's a beautiful color against your skin," he added until he saw her sexy periwinkle-blue lace panties and garter belt. "I like it when a woman coordinates."

She laughed, more so she could get rid of some more nervous butterflies that fluttered in her belly.

"Hold your dress up," he said.

Again, she followed his orders while he reached into his back pocket and removed a condom. They were really going to do this out here on the restaurant's rooftop. Something wicked shivered down her spine and caused her clit to start pounding hard in time to her racing heartbeat.

"Now come back over here and climb back onto my lap," he said.

She glanced around, briefly wondering if anyone could see them from another roof or what would happen if their waiter came back upstairs. Beverly glanced back over at Lucius, her eyes locking with his. While watching the unmistakable passion flicker in his hazel eyes, she stepped closer and then straddled his hips.

Lucius slid the bottom of her panties over to the side and then sighed in ecstasy when she lowered onto his hard erection. It still amazed him how her body seemed to fit him like a glove, and when she began to move he was in serious danger of his eyes rolling out of his head.

Beverly didn't know how it was possible, but she was definitely having trouble getting air into her lungs. Lucius filled her thoroughly and completely.

"Oh, baby. I can't tell you how much I've missed you," Lucius panted, gripping her butt and helping her slam back down on his dick in a good even rhythm. "Pull your breasts out for me."

Still rocking her body, Beverly unhooked the pin that held the one strap on her dress together and allowed it to fall and pool at her waist.

Lucius's mouth watered at the sight of strapless periwinkle bra. When she pulled her full breasts from their cups, he quickly leaned forward and sucked in her marble-sized nipples.

Beverly shuddered and quaked and before long, she felt her own eyes begin to roll to the back of her head. Nearing her first orgasm her rhythm started to slow so Lucius found himself thrusting his hips up harder and faster. "That's it, baby," he panted. "You coming?"

"Y-yeeeesss. Please don't stop."

"I don't plan on stopping, baby." He hammered away while fighting for control himself. He didn't want to come before her, but it was looking like it was going to be a nail-biter to the finish line. Lucius could already feel his toes curling again—a dangerous sign.

"Ooooh, Lucius. Baaabbbeeeee."

"That's right, baby. Let yourself go," he urged. "Ahhh." He bit his lower lip.

Tiny sparks started shooting off in Beverly's head a second before her body started tingling and convulsing. "Oooh, baby. I'm coming."

Hell. So am I!

Beverly finally let herself go as she screamed out his name. Two seconds later, Lucius wrapped an arm around her body tightly and growled with his head planted in the valley between her breasts.

Collapsing against him, Beverly finally filled her lungs with the night's sweet oxygen. When she was finally able to speak, she said, "You're right. Dessert is the best part of the meal."

Luicus laughed and slapped her on the butt. "Let me get you out of here so I can really show you what you've been missing."

Chapter 14

Why did sex with Lucius Gray feel so much like making love?

This was the question that kept racing through Beverly's mind as her supposed *no-strings attached* lover continued to bump and grind in between her legs, all the while stirring up her emotions and eroding her sanity. Never in her life had a man expertly and consistently known when and how to work all of her G-buttons. It was as if he'd stolen her body's owner's manual and studied it inside and out.

Just like their rooftop extravaganza, the presidential suite at the Four Seasons Hotel turned out to be a hopeless romantic's dream: candles, music and red and yellow rose petals sprinkled everywhere. But the main attraction was the huge king-size bed with the leather-upholstered headboard. That was where they now continued to work out and exorcise their sex demons.

Sweat made their beautiful brown bodies feel like silk and it also made it easier for Lucius to glide so deep into her, it felt as if he was bumping up against her heart. Enraptured, Beverly was unaware that tears leaked from the slits of her closed eyes. All she knew was that she had never felt pleasure like this with anyone else in her entire life.

"What are you crying for, baby?" Lucius whispered and then kissed the tracks of her tears.

She shook her head instead of answering and by her hip movements urged him not to stop.

Still concerned, he asked, "Am I hurting you, baby?"

Was he crazy? Couldn't he see how good he was making her feel—how he'd easily abolished the concrete wall that she'd spent years building around her heart?

Lucius's hips stopped moving, causing Beverly to panic and claw at his back. "N-no. Don't stop!" she begged.

"All right, baby. I got you." He started his slow grind again while Beverly moaned her relief. "Is this what you wanted?"

No. This was what she needed, but she couldn't get the words out. The only thing she could do was squirm, whimper and cry.

"Don't you ever leave me like that again," he whispered hoarsely in her ear. "You hear me, baby?" For emphasis he buried himself balls-deep into her silky wetness, causing a baritone moan to resonate from within her soul. "There won't be any more of that creeping out while I'm sleeping nonsense. You got that, baby?"

She nodded vigorously.

"Let me hear you say it."

Beverly struggled to string words together for a complete sentence. "I—I won't…"

"Creep out in the middle of the night," Lucius aided her.

"C-creep out in the…m-middle of the n-night," she finished, just as her thighs began to shake and a wonderful pressure at the tip of her clit started pounding out of control.

"Look at me, baby," he ordered.

Her long lashes fluttered open and their eyes locked. The passion that stared back at her threatened to consume her. However, there was nothing that could make her turn away at that moment.

Lucius took her arms and stretched them over her head while he pounded in and out, his hips alternating from side to side without mercy. When her orgasm was just seconds from detonating, the moaning stopped while she held her breath in anticipation.

Then…it hit and her voice came back to full power, screaming his name and not giving a damn if the people in the next room heard her or not. Lucius quickly followed her over the edge of sanity, exploding so hard he shook from his very foundation. He collapsed, panting and raining tiny kisses across her fevered brow.

How on earth does this woman keep doing this to me? He slid down next to her and pulled her close. To his amazement, she was already knocked out fast asleep. He smiled, his male ego expanding. As he stared down at her from his lofty cloud of pride, he drank in her glowing and angelic profile. *She's so beautiful,* he marveled, feeling his heart muscles squeeze.

Lucius thought about his pledge for them to have a no-strings-attached nonrelationship and recognized the joke it was. He was already attached; he had been from the first moment he saw her stroll into that bar wearing that knockout red dress. If he was really truthful with himself, he would admit that he had fallen hard for Beverly Turner and that he was tangled in so many strings that he could barely breathe.

He leaned down and brushed a butterfly kiss against the tip of her nose. This was peace and serenity like he'd never known and now that he had her back in his life he knew at that moment that he would move hell and high water to keep her in it.

Beverly stirred in his arms and once again her eyes fluttered open.

"Hello, sleepyhead."

She smiled sheepishly. "Did I pass out?"

He nodded and tweaked her cheek. "Maybe you overexerted yourself."

Beverly laughed.

"What?"

"You're fishing for a compliment," she accused.

"Who, me?" Lucius pressed a hand against his chest in mock innocence. "I was just making an observation. You know, judging by the amount of sweat and hollering you were doing, I said to myself, 'Self, if Beverly don't slow down, she's going to overexert herself.'"

She popped him on the shoulder. "You're not funny."

"No?" He frowned. "Maybe there's something wrong with your funny bone. I should take a look at it." Lucius pulled back the top sheet and pretended to look under her breasts.

"What are you doing? My funny bone isn't under there."

"Shhh. I'm in charge of the inspection here." He tickled her side and giggled. "Oooh. Maybe your funny bone is over here." Lucius moved over and placed a kiss against the curve of her hip.

Beverly sighed.

"Nope. That's not it." He slipped down farther and could

tell by the way her stomach muscles tightened that she was holding her breath, waiting for his next move. Smiling, he dipped two fingers inside the fat folds of her pussy. Her wet walls quivered around his fingers. "Maybe it's here." He kissed those same fat lips. "Should I check inside here, baby?"

Beverly managed a weak whispered reply. "Y—yes."

Without missing a beat, Lucius scooped her firm thighs into his hands and then began to lick each side of her throbbing clit.

Beverly shook and moaned.

"Oh, this is some good candy here," he praised. "You can give a brother a sugar high."

She smiled as she squeezed her big breasts together and pinched her nipples.

Lucius's long tongue slithered and snaked its way inside her, lapping up her sweet juices until her thick, chocolate thighs began quaking again around his head.

"Oooh, Lucius. You're going to make me come again," she moaned.

He licked harder, faster.

"Aaaaaaaah." She swirled her hips, grinding her wetness against his open mouth.

Lucius waited until he knew that she was hot and ready, then slipped two fingers inside her moist cave.

Beverly's nails clawed at the soft sheets. New tears surfaced and rolled from her eyes as bliss blossomed and enfolded her. Before she knew it, she was crying—*really* crying.

Lucius glided up her tall body, gathered her in his arms and rained more kisses across her face. "Shhh, baby. Don't cry, it's going to be all right," he promised.

Would it? She didn't know anymore. Beverly curled

under his shoulder and washed his chest with her tears. Why was she crying? She wished she knew. Maybe it was nothing or maybe it was everything. Tomorrow she would probably hate herself for this—to allow herself to be this vulnerable with Lucius, but for right now, she didn't care. She just wanted him to hold her.

It was a long time before her tears subsided. When they did, she was both surprised and relieved that there didn't seem to be any awkwardness hanging in the air between them. However, something did change—something small and invisible that was growing stronger by the second.

The question was whether or not she could handle it. She closed her eyes and tried to block it out, but love nipped at her heart, determined that it would not be denied. *No strings. No strings,* she chanted inside her head. But she imagined that there was another voice, laughing at her futile attempt.

Beverly vowed that she would hang on, by the tips of her nails, if need be.

I won't fall in love. I won't fall in love. Her tears started up again.

"Awww, sweetheart. Don't do that." He started kissing away her tears again.

She clung to him and said without thinking, "Make love to me." *What? What did I just say?*

"Yes, baby. Anything you want." Lucius maneuvered around, slid on a new condom and entered her so deftly and smoothly that she came on the spot. When she caught her breath again, she locked gazes with him. She was getting accustomed to seeing that same hunger and passion in his eyes and she was loving it as much as she was afraid that she was falling in love with him.

Beverly pushed and then rolled him over to take the top position.

Lucius licked his fat, juicy lips as he watched her wind her hips. Her first strokes were so slow and deep that even though he didn't say anything, his twisting facial expressions said it all. She picked up speed, causing her round butt to slap hard against his legs and hips. Suddenly, he wasn't so quiet, sucking and hissing through his gritted teeth.

Beverly knew he was on the brink of exploding, but was also struggling to prolong the moment. She smiled and pounded down on him without mercy. As far as she was concerned, she was in control of this groove and she wanted him to come when she wanted him to come.

Lucius was swept away at how good Beverly looked gliding up and down, and then grinding every other stroke. Her full breasts jiggled and bounced and were causing a brother to get dizzy. But he knew that he had to give up the ghost when he felt that familiar tingle in his toes. He reached around and filled his hand with her bouncing booty. Soon he was moaning and groaning so loud, he wouldn't be surprised if people thought there was a wounded animal in the room.

Beverly's wet walls started to contract and before he knew it, they were both crying out to the heavens and then floating somewhere in the clouds.

Chapter 15

For two bliss-filled weeks, Lucius and Beverly continued with their farce of a *no-strings-attached* relationship and everyone working at Hoops took notice of Beverly's remarkable change. Not only would she sing "I'm Every Woman" but she had added "Tell Me Something Good" and "Sexual Healing" to her musical repertoire. Bottom line, she felt good—damn good—and there was no point in pretending otherwise. Of course, now her good mood brought out the green monster in her friends.

"Now I'm just flat-out jealous," Clarence admitted after watching Beverly flit around the store, smiling grandly to all the customers that flowed through her door. "I know I said I wanted you to relax, but I don't know if I can handle all this saccharine, bubble-gum B.S."

"I guess that means you still haven't found yourself a

new man?" Beverly asked, ignoring his attempt to rain on her parade.

"Don't worry about me, sweetheart. I'm just sitting on the bench for a couple innings. I'll be back in the game before the seventh-inning stretch. You can believe that."

"Well, I think it's wonderful," Leslie said, refolding a stack of sweaters at one of the display tables. "Life is too short to be miserable. If your man is giving you what you need, then more power to you."

Beverly held up her hands. "Well, I wouldn't exactly call him *my* man. More like my very good friend with fringe benefits."

"Don't you mean French benefits?" Clarence started making annoying kissing noises.

Beverly didn't break her stride, but flashed him the bird for his heckling. "I don't know how many times I've told you that green is *not* your color."

Clarence rolled his eyes. "Whateva. My next man is gonna be fine and is going to put your big-dick playboy to shame."

"Clarence!" Beverly stomped her foot. "Boy, I have customers in here," she hissed.

He glanced around the store. "Please, we all grown folks up in here."

Leslie snickered.

"Don't you have customers today?" Beverly asked.

"Not until two o'clock—and don't change the subject," he warned. "We're in the middle of stirring your fruit punch right now. Are you and Mr. Lover-Lover spending Thanksgiving together tomorrow or are you going to your parents'?"

Beverly's cheeks flushed guiltily. "Well, Lucius has mentioned that since his ex-wife was taking his daughter to Boston that he would be alone for the holiday."

Clarence and Leslie shot a look at each other.

"What?" Beverly asked.

"You know when you start spending the holidays together it means you taking things to another level."

Beverly glanced away. It felt as if she and Lucius were advancing to another level, despite her having a few conflicting emotions.

Clarence crept over to her, his eyes narrowing with suspicion. "Do you *want* things to move to a new level?"

She shrugged. "I don't know. I'm just going with the flow right now."

"Oh, my God," he gasped, pressing a hand to his chest. "You're really feeling this brother." Suddenly, Clarence threw his arms around Beverly. "I was just playing before, but, girl, I'm so proud of you taking this huge step."

"Whoa. Whoa. Whoa." She tossed up her arms and wiggled out of his embrace. "I didn't say all of that. I'm just taking baby steps."

Clarence's neck swiveled back. "Baby steps? Girl, you slept with him on your first date—well, I don't even know if you can call it a date."

"Will you please keep your voice down?" Beverly hissed. After another glance around, she said, "Contrary to what you might believe, I don't want everybody to know my business."

"Please. You just scared that everybody is going to think that you're a ho. Screw 'em. Hos need love, too."

Beverly pressed two fingers against the center of Clarence's head and pushed him away from her. "Boy, you're too much."

"All right. All right. I'm happy for you. I think it's great that you're diving back into the pool of love." He held up a hand before she could protest. "I know. I know. You didn't say anything about being in love, but—" he locked gazes with her "—it's written all over your face whether you want to admit it or not."

The bell above the shop's door jingled. Beverly turned and then immediately her face lit up. "Kyra!" She rushed over and embraced her friend. "What are you doing here?"

"I came by to see you, silly. And to show you this— *bam!*" She threw out her hand where a white diamond solitaire sparkled back at them. "Your girl is engaged."

Beverly's eyes bulged. "Oh, my God."

Clarence literally hip-bumped Beverly out of the way. "Ooooh, girl. Who the hell are you marrying—Michael Jordan or some damn body? Leslie, come look at this chick's rock."

"Isn't it gorgeous?" Kyra giggled.

Beverly stood with her mouth hanging open. "You and…"

"Terrence," Kyra supplied. "He popped the question. Can you believe it? After all these years, we're actually going to get married. Bev, it was sooo sweet, he proposed to me at the same exact spot where we met ten years ago at Hollington." Her bubbling excitement was infectious.

"That's wonderful," Beverly finally said, opening her arms and embracing her friend. "I'm so happy for you."

"Thanks. My other good news is that Terrence accepted the coaching and teaching job at Hollington. So we'll be staying right here in Atlanta." Kyra stepped back and smiled at her. "I keep pinching myself every ten minutes to make sure I'm not dreaming."

Knowing the history between Kyra and Terrence caused Beverly's heart to overflow with joy for her friend.

Clarence beamed. "Sounds like love was all up in the air at that college reunion shindig. What—this makes the third engagement?" he asked, looking to Beverly for confirmation. "I wonder if my hair college throws reunion parties. Maybe I'm missing out on something."

"Speaking of which," Kyra said, beaming. "Did you hear about Tamara Hodges and Micah Ross?"

Beverly folded her arms. "Yeah. We read about it in *Luster* magazine."

"Stunning, huh?" Kyra giggled. "No doubt Micah is going to throw her some fabulous wedding out in La La Land, but I tossed in a good word for Hoops to Tamara. So don't be surprised if she drops in."

Beverly blinked. "I don't do wedding gowns."

"Not the gown, silly. But for her engagement party dress. The dress will get a lot of attention since Micah is a big-time mover and shaker in the music industry."

Beverly lit up. "Thanks, girl."

"C'mon. You know I'll always have your back. Plus, I was hoping by hooking you up it will mean I'll get a little discount on my own engagement party dress?"

"I'll do better than that. Your dress with be my wedding gift to you."

"Aww. Thank you."

They shared another hug and then Beverly led Kyra to the alteration room, where she could take down her friend's measurements and discuss her vision for what type of dress she'd like for a quaint engagement party. Leslie brought back a couple of flutes of champagne and before Beverly knew it, two hours had passed and Kyra had to go.

"'Bye, I'll see you in a couple of weeks," Beverly said, waving.

As Kyra was leaving Clarence was returning to the store.

"Finished with your afternoon appointment?" Beverly asked.

"Mmm-hmm," he said, following her to her office with a slick smile.

She stopped, not liking his calculating smile. "What?"

"What-what?" He played dumb.

Beverly folded her arms beneath her chest and waited him out.

Clarence finally relented. "I just keep thinking that with so much reunion love in the air that *possibly* it's infected one more couple."

She quickly caught his meaning. "I'm *not* in love."

He folded his arms to match her stance. "Methinks thou protest too much."

"Mr. Gray, I have a Kevin Stayton on line one," Maggie chirped over Lucius's speakerphone.

Surprised, Lucius pulled his nose out of the piles of legal briefs and picked up the phone. "Kevin! How the hell are you?"

"I'm doing good, man. I'm doing good," Kevin said. "I know it's been a minute since the reunion and when we talked about the CHRIS Kids Foundation."

Lucius eased back in his chair. He had forgotten about Kevin's request about helping the charity foundation.

"I'm sorry about taking so long getting back to you, but things have been a little hectic dealing with wedding preparations."

"Hey, it's cool. I completely understand. I've been meaning to congratulate on your pending nuptials. That was really cool taking the stage at the reunion dance party.

I kept telling Beverly that something was going on between you two."

Kevin's deep laughter rumbled over the line. "Yeah. I don't think I'll forget Chloe's stunned face when my proposal finally sunk in. Priceless."

"I'm happy for you, man." Lucius was unprepared for a sudden stream of fantasy images of him dropping on one knee before Beverly. Only problem was he suspected her response wouldn't be anything like Chloe Jackson's at the reunion dance party, but more like a screaming heroine in a horror movie. For now, he had to settle for the pretense of a *no-strings-attached* relationship, despite the fact that they practically saw each other every day now. In fact, she spent more nights at his place than hers. A lot of times, she used the excuse that his house was a lot closer to her shop than her own, but he knew the truth. She was starting to care for him—maybe even love him—but she was nowhere near ready to admit it.

Lucius forced himself to concentrate on Kevin's phone call. He was more than happy to agree to do pro bono work for the CHRIS Kids Foundation. He'd heard a lot of good things about the charity based there in Atlanta and was extremely impressed at Kevin's passion and dedication to the group. After the call, he glanced at his watch and smiled when he saw that it was exactly five o'clock.

"Time to go." He quickly tossed a few case files into his briefcase and grabbed his suit jacket.

Maggie entered the office, carrying a new stack of legal briefs, but then stopped and stared at him. "Leaving?"

"Yep. I'm calling it a day," he said, wondering whether he should stop by the store and surprise Beverly with a home-cooked meal tonight.

His secretary set the briefs down on his desk and then crossed her arms. "All right. What gives?" she asked cautiously. "I've never known you to just work forty hours a week."

"And if I recall, you always said that I worked too much."

"And since when do you take my advice?"

He walked from behind his desk. "Heeey, better late than never, right?"

Maggie shook her head as she followed him out of the office. "*Something* is going on with you—I'm inclined to believe that it may be a woman."

"Are you now?" he said, refusing to sate her curiosity.

"It's that or you jumped the fence and are seeing a man," she goaded.

"Hmmm." Lucius refused to take the bait, and pressed a button for the elevator.

"Oh, you're good," she said.

Lucius chuckled as the elevator's door slid open. "Good night, Maggie."

"This isn't over," she warned, laughing.

In the parking deck, Lucius hopped into his Crossover and turned over the engine. Lauryn Hill's CD was still in his CD player, which only boosted his good mood. Unfortunately, that all ended when his cell phone rang five minutes later. "Hello, Erica," he said flatly.

"What time are you going to be home?" she asked without preamble.

He frowned, recognizing an Erica trap when he heard one. "Why?"

"Because I'm bringing *your* daughter over. Is that a problem?"

"Of course not," he said, insulted.

"Good—because you're keeping her through the Thanksgiving holiday."

"All right." Lucius waited for an explanation, but when clearly there wasn't one forthcoming, he asked, "I thought you were taking her to Boston?"

"Well, I'm not. *Okay?* There's no reason why she can't stay with you. You're her father, remember?"

Lucius drew a deep breath and counted to ten. "I'm not complaining about keeping her, Erica. I just wanted to know why there was a change in plans. I'd love to have her for the holidays. I just wanted to know—"

"Great. It's settled," she snapped. "Now what time will you be home?"

"I—I guess in about ten minutes. Why?"

"I'll see you in ten minutes." She hung up.

Lucius pulled the phone from his ear and stared at it. "What the hell was all that about?" He didn't have to wait long to find out, because Erica and Ruby were standing on his doorstep waiting when he pulled into his driveway.

"Daddy!" Beaming, Ruby raced over to him as he climbed out of his vehicle.

"Hey, baby." He swept his arm around her and gave her a big hug. "How are you doing?" He kissed her on the cheek and then carried her on his hip as he walked to the door, where he nodded to his ex-wife. "Erica."

She didn't respond to the greeting. "I'll be back Monday to pick her up."

"All right." Lucius nodded but found it strange that it seemed like she was going out of her way not to look at him.

"Goodbye, baby." Erica leaned over and kissed Ruby's cheek and then raced to her car.

Lucius stared, trying to figure out what had just

happened. He and Erica weren't always on the best of terms but he couldn't think of a reason for her just treating him like he was something stuck on the bottom of her shoe all of a sudden. He watched as she started her car and jetted out of the driveway like a bat out of hell.

"Daddy, are we going to have turkey or ham for Thanksgiving?"

He smiled and winked at his daughter. "We can have whatever you like."

"I want ham!"

"Then ham it is!" Lucius turned around and stuck his key into the front door when he remembered something. "I hope you don't mind, but Daddy is also going to have a friend over as well."

"A girlfriend?" she inquired, perking up.

"I guess you could say that."

Chapter 16

Beverly spent Wednesday night at her house, doing something she hadn't done in a long time: baking. It was the least she could do since Lucius had insisted on doing all the major cooking for their Thanksgiving meal and her mother had always taught her to never show up to such things empty-handed. For the occasion she made one pumpkin pie and one pecan pie.

Now that it was getting close to the time for her to head out to Lucius's place, she found herself getting nervous about this *surprise* that Lucius had hinted about last night on the phone. Mainly because Clarence had also spent the last twenty-four hours popping all this nonsense about their spending time together on a major holiday meant that her and Lucius's relationship was moving to the next level. Was this what Lucius was thinking, too—and did this *surprise* have something to do with that?

Lord, she hoped not.

If Beverly had her way their relationship would remain on this level—cruise control. She didn't ask too much from him and he didn't ask too much from her. Just sex.

Of course they had been spending an awful lot of time together lately, but that was normal for new lovers. Eventually that would dial back and they would just see each other whenever the need or mood arose.

So you wouldn't mind if he started seeing other women?

Beverly's heart squeezed when the unbidden question floated across her head as she wrapped her pies in aluminum foil. *Of course not,* she lied to herself. *Why should I care if he decides to see other women?* She clenched her jaw as her blood pressure surely climbed while thinking about Lucius holding another woman the same way he held her—or kissed her.

Turning, Beverly crossed her arms and leaned back against the counter while her emotions churned like a tornado inside of her. What the hell was going on with her? Why was she getting upset about a fictional woman?

"Get it together, Beverly," she whispered and shook her head. "You're getting ahead of yourself."

After a few deep breaths, she felt her nerves settle down. Surely she was blowing things out of proportion. For all she knew Lucius wanted to surprise her with some special dish he made and nothing more. He hadn't given her any hint that he was thinking their relationship was anything more than what he declared.

That's not true.

Beverly was suddenly flooded with memories of words exchanged in bed. How many times had he asked her whom she belonged to or hold out giving her the orgasm she craved until she admitted that they were more than friends? *That was just sex talk,* she told herself, but suddenly she wasn't so sure.

The phone rang, startling her. Grateful for a reprieve from her own troubled thoughts, Beverly rushed to answer it.

"Happy Thanksgiving."

Lucius's deep baritone put an instant smile on Beverly's face. "Happy Thanksgiving."

"What time can I expect you to come over?" he asked.

"Oh, probably about an hour," she estimated.

"Good. I should have everything done by then."

"Sooo, hmmm…can I get a hint about this surprise now?" Beverly asked.

Lucius chuckled. "Nope. You're going to have to wait."

"Ugh!"

"Patience is a virtue," he said, laughing. "Now hurry up and get your butt over here. I think I fixed enough food to feed half of Georgia."

"All right. See you in a few." She hung up the phone and then raced upstairs to finish getting ready. But when she reached the top of the stairs, her feet slowed when her gaze skittered to the closed door at the other end of the hallway. For the past few weeks, she had been flying high between work and her new love affair, and for the first time in years, she'd almost forgotten… *No. I'll never forget,* she vowed, as she walked toward that closed door.

When she reached out and her hand wrapped around the cold brass knob, a renewed wave of sadness engulfed her—so much that she resisted pushing the door open. What was the point? Her eyes glossed as she released the doorknob and stepped back.

"Get it together," she whispered brokenly. Why was she insisting on punishing herself? Beverly turned away from the door just as a few tears skipped down her face. Why was she so determined to keep punishing herself? Why couldn't she just move on?

She closed her eyes, drew in a deep breath and focused on something that made her feel good. It didn't take long for Lucius's image to surface and a wonderful calm to settle over her. When she opened her eyes, she knew beyond a shadow of a doubt that she was in trouble.

Lucius tried and tried but finally had to give up on his daughter's hair. He just couldn't seem to get it to do what he wanted it to do. "How about we just wear it down today?" he asked.

"Okay," Ruby said, excited and anxious for him to stop pulling on her head. She grabbed the brush from his hand and quickly started to repair the damage he'd caused. In a couple of strokes, she returned to looking normal. "We need to curl the ends. Do you have a curling iron?"

He blinked. "Can't say that I do."

She pouted her lips.

"But it looks fine the way that it is," he assured her. The last thing he wanted to do was try to work something hot and electrical in her hair. With his luck, he would burn half her face and head and people at the hospital emergency room would be looking upside his head like he was a child abuser or something.

"But I want to look nice when I met your girlfriend," Ruby whined.

"What are you talking about?" Lucius said, astonished. "You look gorgeous. Look at you in that dress." He turned her around to face the bathroom mirror. "Beverly is going to take one look at you and think that you're some fairy-tale princess."

Ruby giggled. "She will not."

"Sure she will. Look at those adorable cheeks." Lucius pinched and wiggled them around. "And that nose." He tweaked it using two knuckles. "I don't think there's a cuter nose in the whole wide world."

Laughing heartily, Ruby tried to get away from her dad, but he was now in a tickling mood and he started attacking her waist and belly. His daughter squealed in a tone that nearly burst his eardrums. A while later during the melee, they became aware of the doorbell ringing.

"I'll get it," they shouted in unison and then took off running through the house.

Lucius could have easily overtaken his daughter, but he shortened his strides and allowed her to beat him down the stairs and to the front door. By the time he caught up with her, she'd opened the door and a stunned Beverly blinked down at his daughter.

"Um, well, hello!" Beverly said after finally finding her voice. "And who might you be?" she asked, smiling.

"I'm Ruby. My dad's daughter."

Beverly laughed. "Ahh. I should have known. You have his eyes."

"Daddy said that you'd like my cheeks and nose."

Lucius smacked a hand against his forehead—but it got worse.

"Are you my dad's girlfriend?" Ruby asked, curious.

Beverly stuttered. "I—I—"

"Why don't we invite her inside the house?" Lucius said, coming to her rescue.

Ruby jumped out of the way and hand-combed her hair back down.

A nervous Beverly crossed the threshold, holding two aluminum-wrapped pies.

"Those smell good," Lucius said, hoping to put her at ease since she looked like a scared rabbit. "Don't they smell wonderful, Ruby?"

"Mmm-hmm." Ruby bobbed her head and slammed the door. As everyone walked toward the kitchen, she tugged her father's hand and said in a loud whisper, "She's pretty, Daddy."

Lucius's chest expanded with pride. "I know," he whispered back.

Beverly blushed as she set her desserts on the kitchen counter. "So I take it that you are my surprise today," Beverly said, beaming.

"Yep." Lucius wrapped an arm around her. "Today I'm sharing this holiday with my two favorite ladies. So let's make this official. Beverly, this is Ruby and Ruby, this is Ms. Beverly."

"Hi!" Ruby enthusiastically waved. "Are you going to marry my dad?"

Beverly tensed.

"Ruby." Lucius tried to hint to his daughter to cut it out.

However, she only frowned and asked, "What's wrong with your eyes, Daddy?"

Beverly giggled. "It's okay, Lucius." She walked over to stand next to Ruby. "Me and your daddy are just good friends."

Technically this was the truth, but Lucius still felt slighted—stung. Apparently his daughter felt the same way, judging by the way her face twisted in a frown.

"Enough of this, ladies," Lucius proclaimed, clapping his hands together. "Why don't you two help me get dinner out on the table?"

Beverly looked relieved. "Sounds good to me."

"Okay," Ruby agreed and then proceeded to follow Beverly around like she was her small shadow. And of course, she chatted away nonstop about everything from the class pet turtle at her school to how her mother and her fiancé had chosen to go to Boston for Thanksgiving without her.

To Lucius's great surprise and relief, Beverly seemed to be a pro when it came to dealing with children. She listened attentively and asked questions that Ruby was only too eager to answer. A casual observer would have thought that the two were lifelong friends the way that they carried on. Once dinner was on the table, everyone took their seats, held hands and said their prayers.

After that, Ruby attacked the ham as if she hadn't eaten in a week.

Beverly was amused.

"She *really* likes ham," Lucius tried to explain.

"So I see." She smiled lovingly at Ruby.

Lucius watched the two of them and his chest expanded with pride. It was the first time in a long while that this table had hummed with laughter and joy. The three of them looked like a real family. He liked the way they looked together and how they interacted with one another and as time rolled on, he found himself wishing that the day wouldn't end. When the football game got started, they piled into the living room with cans of root beer, Ruby's favorite, and got ready to cheer on the Dallas Cowboys against the Pittsburgh Steelers.

When the Cowboys made their first touchdown, Beverly

hopped up and taught Ruby a cheer from her old cheerleading days. Ruby loved anything that involved her shaking her butt and acting semi-grown. On the second touchdown, his girls forced him off the couch and jostled him to participate.

Up and down, our team don't mess around,
Because we're the best from the east to the west.
And when our team is up, you're down.
Go Cowboys!

There were a couple of snaps and pops in there Lucius couldn't quite pull off, which sent Ruby and Beverly into hysterical laughter.

It was a great day—one Lucius knew that he would never forget.

Promptly at 9:30 p.m., Ruby finally reached the point of exhaustion and passed out curled up on Beverly's lap. While she slept, Beverly couldn't stop smiling and stroking the girl's long and tousled hair. The child was such an angel that she'd easily won Beverly's heart the moment she introduced herself as her father's daughter.

"You two look good together," Lucius whispered, strolling into the living room. "I think Ruby really likes you," he observed.

"I think I really like her, too," Beverly admitted softly. "You have a beautiful child."

"Thanks." He walked over and gently scooped Ruby out of Beverly's lap. "I better go put her to bed." Ruby rolled up against her father's chest without stirring and he quickly strolled out of the living room and headed up the stairs.

Beverly continued smiling in his wake, thinking how

this holiday was the best one she'd had in a long while. But then she remembered the mess in the dining room and kitchen and decided that she should help Lucius clean up.

When he returned downstairs a few minutes later, he found her in the kitchen loading up the dishwasher. "You don't have to do that," he said, walking in with a few more plates. "You're company."

"I don't mind," Beverly admitted. "Besides, this will go by faster if we both do it."

Lucius apparently wasn't going to look a gift horse in the mouth and didn't protest any further. Together they busted suds, loaded the dishes, wrapped leftovers, took out the garbage and cleaned all of the countertops. Two hours later, the place was spotless and they congratulated each other on a job well done.

"It's late. I better be heading home," Beverly said, stretching and rubbing the muscles on the side of her neck.

"Go?" He frowned and eased behind her so he could take over massaging her neck and shoulders. "I don't want you to go."

Beverly tried to respond, but Lucius's strong hands were performing some kind of voodoo magic, causing her to become as limp as a wet noodle. "Oooh, goodness, that feels good."

"You like that, baby?" He leaned down and brushed his lips just below her right earlobe.

Despite her exhaustion, Beverly's body tingled in response.

"It's too late for you to be out on the road," Lucius whispered. "You know there's a spike in crazy people on the roads during these long holiday weekends."

"But what about Ruby?" she asked weakly.

"She's asleep." His hands slid down her shoulders, changed directions, then roamed up her flat belly and cupped her large breasts.

Beverly moaned; her panties dampened. "What if she wakes up?"

"She won't."

"She could."

Lucius chuckled. "Then we'll have to make sure that we're extra quiet." He squeezed her breasts; his fingers rotated her hard nipples through her blouse and bra.

Beverly's knees buckled, forcing her to lean back against Lucius and bump up against his hard erection. Suddenly, she couldn't remember what the hell they were talking about. Her hips took over as she grinded back against his dick, loving the cheap thrill that it gave her.

"Go ahead, baby. Work it out," he panted, letting her do what it took to get off.

It wasn't long before she worked herself up into such a frenzy that she wanted more than this sexual appetizer.

Lucius easily read her mind and whispered, "Let's go upstairs. In the morning you can just sneak to one of the guest bedrooms before Ruby wakes up."

Problem solved, Beverly took his hand and damn near dragged him up the stairs. He chuckled softly at her impatience. On the top floor, they held their breath and crept on the tips of their toes past Ruby's room. Of course it seemed like every sound was super magnified, especially when Lucius turned the knob to his bedroom and the door hinges screeched like nails down a blackboard.

They both gritted their teeth and waited expectantly for Ruby to stir.

Nothing.

Beverly and Lucius glanced at each other, relieved, and then continued their tiptoe adventure into the bedroom. Once inside, they braced themselves again when he had to close the door behind them. After that was done, they waited a few more seconds before turning around, grinning like two thieves getting away with the crime of the century.

"Come here, baby," he whispered and wrapped an arm around her thick waist.

Beverly glided into his arms and welcomed his hungry kiss. She drank in his heady, sweet taste. She moaned softly as his hands worked quickly to unbutton her blouse, which he then slid off her shoulders. With a snap of his wrist, her bra popped open and joined her top that pooled around her feet.

"Oh, let me taste these titties," Lucius said, dropping his head lower and sucking a fat nipple into his mouth.

Instantly, her eyes rolled to the back of her head. She struggled to keep the noise down as he squeezed, licked and sucked her to paradise. The rest of their clothes were removed in a blurred fury and the next thing she knew, she was being pressed into the center of his firm, king-size mattress.

In the six weeks they'd known each other, Lucius had learned all of Beverly's hot buttons and he now took his time pushing each and every one of them while she writhed and moaned as softly as she could. When that started to become too hard for her, Lucius flipped her onto her back and instructed her to bite into the pillow—which she readily did when he entered her from behind.

Lucius rained kisses on the back of her shoulders and down the center of her spine, all the while slapping his hips against her firm, round ass. As much as his body felt like home to her, Beverly remained amazed how much he filled her up. To drive her even crazier, he reached around her hip and ran the pads of his fingers along the tip of her throbbing clit.

She nearly screamed out loud.

"Shhhh," he urged as he continued to pound away. "We don't want to have to stop this groove now, do we, baby?"

"N—no," she moaned.

"Does this feel good, Bev? Huh? You like how I work your body, baby?"

"Y—yeeessss."

"That's what I thought. Down there talking about going home. You knew I wasn't going to let you go without my dessert." He started to swing his hips from side to side. "Now didn't you?"

"Oooooh."

"Didn't you, baby?" he insisted. "You know you belong to me, right? I can have you anytime I want, can't I?"

"Ooooh."

Lucius stopped. "What—I can't get this anytime I want?"

Beverly's eyes flew wide in panic. "Baby," she whined, thrusting her hips back, trying to get him continue.

He made one long stroke. Stopped. "Can I have this anytime I want?"

"Yes, yes," she panted, climbing on her knees and gliding back on his long dick. She wanted more—needed more.

"Look at you," Lucius murmured. "Work it, baby." He smacked and squeezed her ass cheeks as she continued to ride him hard and deep. "Oooh, yeah. That's my girl."

Beverly glanced back over her shoulder, watched him as his face twisted and contorted with ecstasy. To turn up the heat, she started rotating her hips.

Lucius growled.

"Shhh," she whispered, smiling. "You don't want to stop this groove now, do you?"

"Come here." He chuckled and forced her to stand up on her knees though they still grinded together. "You play too much," he moaned in her ear, still working her clit and thrusting into her warm wetness.

A low heat simmered in Beverly's belly as stars started to blink behind her eyes. Lucius stroked with all he had, causing a glorious friction to tip her over the edge. Her thighs trembled, her breath thinned.

"You coming, baby?"

She wanted to answer but only managed to nod while her gasping started to heighten.

Mindful of who was sleeping just across the hall, Lucius was forced to place his hands over her mouth. However, Beverly responded by sucking on his fingers, while he continued to knock the air from her lungs. Two more pumps and Beverly quivered and convulsed, her orgasm causing a kaleidoscope of colors to spin behind her eyes.

Lucius followed, his explosion marrying their souls together to the point that neither could tell where one of them started and where the other ended. Hot and sweaty, they collapsed back onto the bed. "God, I love you," he whispered raggedly, peppering more kisses against her back.

No answer.

"Beverly?" He leaned over and saw that she had once again fallen fast asleep. Lucius smiled, kissed her shoulder and snuggled up against the curve of her back, and allowed sleep to claim him.

Once his breathing settled and evened out, Beverly's eyes fluttered open as tears streamed from the corners of her eyes and soaked her pillow.

Chapter 17

The four-day holiday weekend turned into a minivacation for Lucius, Beverly and Ruby. First thing Friday morning, after Beverly snuck down to the guest bedroom before Ruby woke, they all gathered for a big breakfast and then got ready to hit the malls for the first shopping day of Christmas.

When Beverly saw the wild concoction Lucius had created on his poor daughter's head, she quickly marched the child back up the stairs and performed an emergency hair makeover with all the pretty bows and ties her mother had packed in her overnight bag. When they reemerged, Ruby strutted like the princess she was in front of her dad.

Lucius gave a thunderous applause and whistled mightily before offering his little girl his arm and escorting her and Beverly out to their vehicle.

Beverly's heart melted at the way Lucius doted on his daughter. It was there for the world to see how much he loved her. This was the kind of man she should've married the first time. As soon as the thought crossed her mind, she had to shake the troubled direction of her thoughts. This was the sort of thinking that could land her in trouble.

All the stores were teeming with anxious and overzealous shoppers. Lucius kept trying to pull them into every electronics store they passed, while Ruby and Beverly sought out toys and clothes stores. Before long, Lucius was reduced to holding bags while his girls kept disappearing behind changing-room doors and then coming out to model different outfits.

Of course he loved every one of them and ended up dropping a fortune before lunchtime.

Saturday and Sunday entailed more shopping with a Disney movie tossed in the mix. But nothing was more adorable to Lucius than watching his daughter attempt to mimic the way Beverly walked or talked—sometimes even the way she laughed or gestured with her hands.

When Beverly caught wind of what Ruby was doing, she appeared flattered and rained a lot of hugs and kisses on her. This was the kind of woman he should have married the first time. She was beautiful, strong and independent. Yet, at the same time, caring, loving and willing to give and share her time.

During the weekend, Lucius kept feeling as if they were already like a small family, and the more he thought about it, the more he liked the idea. The truth of the matter was that he loved waking up every morning curled up with Beverly. When she wasn't around, he couldn't stop thinking about her. And when she *was* around, he couldn't keep his hands off of her.

They were a perfect fit in every way—but he was still

sensing her trying to resist the inevitable. Every time he would mention the word *love,* she would either pretend not to hear him or conveniently fall asleep. Frankly, he was on to her, but he was willing to let it slide—for now.

"Well, well. Look who decided to come back to work," Clarence said when Beverly finally strolled into Hoops Monday afternoon.

"What? I knew the girls had everything under control," Beverly said, flashing a smile at Leslie as she sauntered toward the back of the store.

Clarence followed, switching his hips and carrying on his arm a gorgeous Fendi B Bag. "Clearly you've forgotten that usually *we* have a standing date every Black Friday," he said, folding his arms and leaning against the door frame of her office.

Beverly's mouth dropped open as her eyes widened to the size of half dollars. "Oh. My. God," she gasped. "Oh, Clarence, I'm so sorry." She blinked and shook her head. "I don't know how on earth I'd forgotten about—"

"I do," he drawled. "I know you're not going to sit up in here and tell me that you weren't over at Mr. Lover-Lover's with your legs wrapped around his waist."

"Clarence, behave."

"I am behaving. You ought to be glad I'm not cussing you out for having me up at four o'clock in the morning freezing my butt off. I was trying to do my patriotic duty in wrecking the hell out of my credit cards and I got stood up." He pressed a hand against his chest. "Nobody stands me up. Then I'm blowing up your cell phone and you don't answer that."

Beverly winced. "I left it charging on my charger at home."

"Hmmph."

"Okay. I'm sorry. I was wrong. I did sort of get caught up with Lucius and Ruby."

"Ruby-who?"

"Ruby. Lucius's daughter."

Clarence moved over to the chair next to her desk. "He introduced you to his daughter?"

"Yeah. Her mother changed her plans at the last minute so he had her this weekend." She smiled. "You should have seen her. She's the most adorable thing. Looks so much like her father."

Clarence said nothing, but eyed her up and down.

"What?" she asked defensively.

"Nothing." He shrugged.

Beverly's eyes narrowed. It was obvious that her friend was lying. "Spit it out."

"It's nothing."

Silence.

"I just find it interesting that you seem comfortable about being around his child. You know…since you've had a hard time dealing—"

"It's not the same thing," she said, cutting him off.

Clarence tossed up his hands, signaling that he was backing off.

Beverly shifted in her chair, annoyed and irritated. But when she thought about Ruby's adorable face, she couldn't help but soften up a little bit. She really did enjoy the time she'd spent with the little girl. In fact, she was flattered by how the child attached herself to her like they were lifelong best friends.

She loved that.

"Well," Clarence said, breaking the silence, "I think it's great. There. I said it. I'm not going to say anything else."

He popped out of his seat and headed toward the door. "Wait. I lied." He turned and faced her. "All jokes aside, I really hope you don't try to mess this up. It's well past time that you move on and embrace whatever happiness you can find in this life. And there's no denying that Lucius Gray makes you very happy."

Lucius had planned on at least working a half day the Monday after Thanksgiving, but Erica never showed to pick up Ruby and he had to revamp his day and take his daughter to school. Finally he hopped up and dialed Erica's number to see what the holdup was, but was further frustrated when she didn't answer at any of her contact numbers.

Still he put up a bright front for Ruby, but secretly started worrying about the court case he'd planned to start preparing for today. Lucius had promised himself that he wouldn't do any office work during his father-daughter time. He had done it once years ago and Erica had made him feel guilty for doing so. Since then, he'd promised that when Ruby was around, those rare times, he would give her his full attention. Today challenged that promise.

"Daddy, you're missing the show!" Ruby shouted from the living room.

"All right. Here I come." He hung up the phone and returned to the great adventures of SpongeBob and Patrick. That's where they remained until five o'clock, when he finally stood and went to make dinner from their Thanksgiving leftovers.

Ruby seemed unfazed by the fact that her mother never showed and just simply returned her pink overnight bag up to her room. "Is Beverly coming home for dinner?" she asked, settling into her chair at the dining-room table.

He smiled into her eager eyes. "Um…I don't know," he answered truthfully. After the extensive time Beverly had spent with them over the weekend, he didn't want to pressure or make her feel obligated to spend more time with Ruby simply because she liked her.

"I like your girlfriend," Ruby said simply. "You should marry her."

Lucius laughed at the way his daughter just cut to the chase. "Why are you so determined to get me hitched?"

She shrugged. "Because I want you to be happy."

Their identical hazel-eyed gazes locked and Lucius's heart overflowed at seeing Ruby's open sincerity. "Thank you, baby." He leaned over and pressed a kiss against her forehead.

His daughter beamed. "So are you going to call her and tell her to come over?"

"How about I call her and *invite* her over?" he amended with a wink.

"Goodie!" She hopped up from the table and raced to retrieve the cordless phone like a future Olympian. "Here you go, Daddy. Call her."

Lucius laughed as he took the phone. "All right. All right. Calm down."

Instead of returning to her chair, Ruby danced and hopped around while chanting, "Call her. Call her."

Relenting to peer pressure, Lucius dialed Beverly's cell phone. "Hello," he said, when she finally picked up, but before he could issue the invitation, Ruby snatched the phone and brokered the offer.

"Hey, Beverly. Do you want to come over?"

Pause.

Ruby's gaze shot up to her father, and he feared that Beverly was politely turning down the offer.

"Pleeeease?"

Lucius reached for the phone.

"Oh, goodie!" Ruby resumed bouncing around. "See you when you get here!" She handed her father the phone back.

"Hello." He checked to see if Beverly was still on the line.

"She's so adorable," Beverly said softly.

"And clearly crazy about you," he said, standing from the table and moving toward the kitchen so that his little girl wouldn't overhear him. "Look, I hope you don't feel pressured to—"

"Don't be silly. I'd love to join you guys for dinner. It'll save me from having to cook something myself."

"So you're just using me for my cooking?"

"For your cooking in the kitchen *and* the bedroom," she teased.

"Awww. I get it." He glanced around and then lowered his voice. "You're just using me for my body."

"You didn't know?"

He sniffed and pretended to be offended. "I was hoping that I'd finally found a woman who loved me for me—for my *mind,* as well as my body."

Beverly laughed.

"I have *feelings,*" Lucius continued dramatically.

"Does that mean that you don't want me to come over?"

"Now. I didn't say *that* exactly."

"That's what I thought," she said.

Lucius laughed. "So what time can we expect you here?"

"I'm leaving the shop now. Give me about twenty minutes."

"All right. We'll see you then." He disconnected the call and started back to the table, where Ruby still bounced around in her chair. When the phone rang,

Lucius snatched it up, thinking it was Beverly again. "Forget something, baby?"

Pause.

"Hello?"

"Lucius?" Erica questioned.

"Oh, there you are." Once again, he turned his back to the dining-room table. "Where in the hell are you? I thought you said that you were coming back today. I missed a whole day at the office."

"Oooh. Poor baby. Did the law office implode without you?"

He took a deep, calming breath. It wasn't going to do any good to try to explain anything to Erica. "Okay. Fine. When are you coming to pick up Ruby?"

Silence.

"Erica?"

"Look, Lucius. Things are complicated right now. Andrew and I didn't go to Boston this past weekend."

Not sure where this was heading, Lucius folded his arms and leaned against the kitchen door. "Okay. So where did you go?"

"Las Vegas," she said. "We eloped."

Silence.

"Lucius?"

"I guess that means that congratulations are in order," he said.

"Th—thank you."

He drew in a deep breath. "Soooo, when do think you'll be coming back?"

Silence.

An icy fear dripped down the center of Lucius's spine. "You *are* coming back, aren't you?"

"Look, Lucius. Andrew isn't ready to be a father right now. And it really bothers him that Ruby looks sooo much like you."

"What?!"

"Hey, don't yell at me," she snapped. "It's not like this is easy for me. I'm not completely turning my back on Ruby. I'm just…*we* need some time alone right now. Sometime down the line, Andrew may adapt to the idea of being a full-fledged stepfather."

"What—she's going to miraculously stop looking like me?" he hissed. "I don't believe this. I can't believe that *you* are just dumping your daughter."

"I am not *dumping* her. I'm leaving her with her father. You are that, you know."

"Stop it, Erica. You're not going to guilt-trip me. This is about you and the cowardly way you are handling this. I'm more than happy to keep Ruby, especially now that I know how her *stepfather* feels."

"It's not that Andrew *hates* her."

"Save it," Lucius snapped. "Just go off and enjoy your new marriage. It sounds like you two deserve each other." He disconnected the call, wanting to scream and throw the phone against the wall.

"Daddy, your food is getting cold," Ruby yelled.

Lucius drew a couple of deep breaths. He couldn't believe this was happening. As of this moment, he was a full-time single father. That meant new schools, day care—and how would this affect his erratic hours at the job?

"Daddy!"

Exhaling a long breath, he forced a smile to his face. "Here I come, baby."

Chapter 18

When Beverly heard about Erica abandoning her child so she could be free to start a new life with her new husband she was just stunned. She couldn't imagine a *mother* deciding to do such a thing. It even forced her to reevaluate some of the things that had gone on in her marriage.

The unfairness.

The injustice.

And poor Lucius was just stunned and tried his best to shield Ruby from all the real drama that was going on between her parents. It was also clear in the next two weeks that Lucius was overwhelmed. Choosing new schools and day care centers were monumental decisions and it pulled at Beverly to see Lucius wrestle with so many tough choices. Ruby on the other hand seemed pleased about the whole arrangement, especially the continued time she spent with Beverly.

In the beginning, Beverly kept telling herself to not get too close. This situation had nothing to do with her. But Ruby, like her father, had crept under her defenses and stolen a piece of her heart whether she liked it or not. By the second week in December, Beverly had gone from the no-strings-attached sex partner to acting and behaving like a member of this small family who laughed at the dinner table and cheered on their favorite football teams on Monday nights. And it was a complete madhouse in the mornings when everyone was trying to get to school and work on time.

As Clarence joked, Beverly was part of the family all but in name. The idea of that both thrilled and frightened her. How did she get here—and so fast? When she questioned herself on why she hadn't just walked away, the answer was so obvious it smacked her in face. She was in this situation because, despite her precautions, she had fallen in love with Lucius Gray.

She loved everything about him. From the way he loved and supported her to the way he sat his daughter on a pedestal. And though he struggled with the toll of suddenly becoming a single full-time father, he went out of his way to hide his distress from his daughter. Although she sometimes missed her mother, Ruby Gray just knew that her father loved and adored her—and that's all that Lucius wanted her to know.

Clarence kept eyeing his friend warily, constantly warning her not to be her own worst enemy. Still there were parts of her that were panicking. She doubted her ability to be able to travel this road to its natural conclusion. And there was no doubt what that conclusion was. Every night, Lucius whispered words of love and now those same words were seeping into their daily phone conversations. The situation both thrilled and terrified her.

What was so wonderful about Lucius was that he seemed to sense her inability to say the words back, even though she went out of her way to make sure that she showed him how she felt every time they fell into each other's arms. But she couldn't get herself to say the words. Saying them would change everything.

She just wasn't ready for that.

At precisely five o'clock, Maggie looked up from her desk to see Lucius calling it a night. "I don't know what's come over you these past couple of months, but I have to admit, I like it."

"Because when I work forty hours that means you do, too?" he asked.

"There is that," she admitted. "Plus, it gives me a complete thrill to know that I was right. A woman is responsible for all of this."

"Only if by woman you mean a certain eight-year-old," Lucius countered, grinning.

"Nuh-uh." Maggie waved a long manicured nail at him. "My husband and I went to the movies yesterday and you'll never guess who we saw sitting just a couple of rows in front of us."

Lucius coughed and pretended to clear his throat.

"Ringing any bells?" she taunted.

"You shouldn't be spying on your boss," he warned playfully and then headed to the elevator bay.

"For what it's worth," she called after him, "I think she's beautiful."

It was a superficial comment, but it still caused Lucius's chest to expand with pride. "Yeah," he acknowledged, "she is."

* * *

Lucius picked up his chattering daughter at precisely 5:30 p.m. from a private day care center. While buckled in the backseat, Ruby decided it was her duty to reeducate her father on his multiplication time tables by using her huge flash cards. When they were getting ready to pass by the Shane Diamond Company, Lucius's foot eased up off of the accelerator. "Baby, do you mind if we take a little detour?"

"Okay," she said absently as she continued to flip through her cards.

After parking and walking hand in hand with his daughter into the large building, Lucius's heart began to flutter.

"Can I help you, sir?" an attractive saleswoman inquired.

Lucius drew in a deep breath. "I'm looking for the perfect engagement ring."

Ruby's head jerked up at her father. "Daddy, are we going to propose to Beverly?"

A large smiled spread across Lucius's face. "Yes, we are, baby. Yes, we are."

Beverly was torn.

She'd told herself that she was going to spend some quiet time alone at home. Give her the chance to step back and clear her mind. But after she'd closed the shop, she started wondering what Ruby and Lucius would be doing that night. So when Lucius called to see if she'd like to join them for dinner at Ruth's Chris Steak House for dinner, she accepted the invitation without missing a beat.

After hanging up, Beverly chastised herself for caving so easily. She wanted her space but she couldn't stay away. What sense did that make?

"That's what love does to you," Clarence said when she explained the situation to him. "Have you thinking you're coming when you're going. You should know this. You've been here before."

That was the wrong thing to say because she had been here before—though it was a little different, she reasoned. David Clark was never as caring and giving as Lucius. Everything was about supporting him and encouraging him with his schooling and then career. And when...

"You're doing it again," Clarence warned.

She looked up. "What?"

"You're thinking about things...people you couldn't change."

She shrugged and started to deny it, but what was the use? Clarence knew her better than anyone. He could smell B.S. a mile away.

"Why can't you just admit that you love him?"

"What does that have to do with anything?"

"Who needs a heart when a heart can be broken?" he inquired.

"Exactly."

Clarence rolled his eyes and chuckled. "Face it, girl. You can't run from love the rest of your life. The past is the past and it's time for you to bury it and move on."

Beverly heard what he was saying and she waited for his message to sink in, but the bottom line still remained: she was scared.

"How's my tie?" Lucius asked his daughter after nervously tying and retying the damn thing about a thousand times.

"Here, let me help." Ruby hopped up onto the edge of

his bed and told him to kneel down so she could wiggle his tie around. "There," she announced. "That's better."

Lucius turned toward the full-length mirror on the back of the closet door and was stunned that indeed his tie was now ramrod-straight. "Weeelll, thanks, sweetheart." He delivered a quick peck against her cheek. "Wish me luck."

"Good luck, Daddy!"

He walked downstairs and thanked Maggie for agreeing to babysit Ruby on such short notice.

"Not a problem. It gives my husband ample opportunity to try to find a good place to stash my Christmas gift." She shrugged. "It won't do him any good. I'm a hound dog when it comes to sniffing out gifts."

"Now why don't I have any trouble believing that?"

They laughed and before Lucius walked out of the door, he gave Ruby explicit directions to be a good girl and to mind Maggie while he was gone. After another kiss goodnight, he was out the door, the weight of the ring heavy in his pocket and on his mind.

Beverly was glad that she'd insisted on meeting Lucius at the restaurant instead of having him pick her up. At least she would have one last out. Of course if Lucius started playing footsies or looked at her a certain way, she could still end up at his place scratching up his back and climbing the walls. When it came to Lucius she was a sex addict.

When she entered the glass doors of Ruth's Chris Steak House, Lucius was already there standing near the hostess stand. When he turned and flashed his beautiful smile at her, her knees weakened and her heart fluttered. *I'm fighting a losing battle with this man.*

He walked over to her and she slid easily into his arms. "Hey, baby. You look beautiful."

"Thank you." She glanced around. "Where's Ruby?"

"Home with a babysitter. It's just you and me tonight. I hope you don't mind."

Beverly smiled. "I guess I'll just have to suffer through."

"Mr. Gray, your table is waiting," the hostess informed him.

Lucius turned while still holding Beverly on his arm. "Shall we?"

"We shall." She allowed him to escort her to their waiting table, smiled when he held out her chair and blushed when he kissed her cheek before walking to his own chair. It was then that she noticed there was something different about his demeanor, something about the way he smiled at her.

Suddenly it felt like a vat of butterflies had broken from their cocoons and started fluttering like mad in the pit of her stomach. Without explanation her palms started to itch and she could hardly sit still in her seat.

Lucius either ignored or didn't notice her fidgeting, but he smiled at their waiter when he appeared with the menus and ran through the night's special.

Beverly hardly heard a word that was said; she just wanted a glass of wine to try to settle her nerves.

"Are you all right?" Lucius asked.

She glanced up and noticed that he and the waiter were staring at her expectantly. "Oh, yes. I was just thinking about all those choices," she lied. Glancing down at the menu, she just randomly picked an entrée number and then smiled tightly when she handed the menu back over to his waiting hand.

Lucius cocked a brow at her. "Are you sure you're all right?"

"Fine," she squeaked and then coughed to clear the growing lump from her throat. Thank God their bottle of wine arrived. She watched almost impatiently as the waiter showed the label to both her and Lucius before uncorking and pouring the damn thing. At the first taste of the heady liquid, she sighed and nearly melted with relief.

Lucius smiled, obviously thinking whatever was troubling her was now over with. "Better?"

"Much." She took another long gulp and drained the rest of her glass.

"You must have been thirsty," he joked.

"Something like that." Beverly averted her eyes. She still had the sneaking suspicion that Lucius was up to something tonight—and she feared that she knew what it was. *Please, God, let me be wrong.*

Lucius didn't know what to make of Beverly's behavior. It was actually setting him on edge, causing him to reevaluate what he wanted to do tonight. First, she had insisted on driving herself to the restaurant and now she seemed to be going out of her way not to meet his gaze. It all made for an uncomfortable start to what he wanted to be a romantic evening.

By the time their meals were delivered to the table, they had already suffered through strained bouts of silence, stiff smiles and sporadic, awkward and choppy conversations.

"Hmmm. This is good," Beverly said.

"Yeah. This place serves the best steaks in town," he offered and then they fell silent again.

It wasn't until Beverly started in on her third glass of wine that she truly began to loosen up and started relating a few funny incidents that had happened in her shop that day. Lucius listened intently, finding her work fascinating, mainly because it was so different from his own profession. He even challenged her by asking whether she'd ever thought about stepping outside of the box and starting her own label.

Beverly loved the fact that Lucius was so interested in her work. It was just another example, in a long list of examples, of how different he was from her ex-husband. *Why can't you stop fighting this?* she asked herself while battling an unexplainable rush of tears. As much as she had shared with him in such a short amount of time, there was still a lot she hadn't—especially the part that haunted her soul.

"Let's make a toast," Lucius said, suddenly lifting his wineglass.

Beverly forced on a smile and followed suit.

"To the past two months. May they only be the beginning to something wonderful."

Was tonight their two-month anniversary? Beverly's hand started to tremble, but she clinked her glass to his in solidarity and added, "Hear, hear."

The rest of their dinner passed by in a blur. Lucius never quite felt the right moment had approached for him to whip out the diamond ring in his pocket. Another idea popped into his mind—something that would perhaps help to relax Beverly. "You know what's just a couple of blocks from here?"

Beverly's gaze shifted up to his in curiosity.

"The downtown Hilton," he supplied. "The place where we met just two months ago tonight." He leaned forward and carefully placed his elbows on the white linen tablecloth. "What do you say that we revisit where the magic started?"

A sparkle finally glittered in Beverly's eyes. The idea definitely had appeal.

"Remember how big and soft their beds were?"

Beverly's brows hiked as she gently bit her lower lip.

He smiled, his voice dropping even lower. "Remember how I had you bend over and grab your ankles?"

She nodded, squirmed in her chair.

"Maybe this time I'll tie you up," he suggested slyly.

From the corner of Beverly's eyes, she saw their server across the way. She literally jumped up from her seat and yelled, "Check, please."

As luck would have it, Lucius and Beverly were able to check into the same room number at the Hilton in downtown Atlanta. And as before, they stumbled into the room pulling and tugging at each other's clothes as if the fate of the world depended on them merging as fast as possible. Yet, the moment Lucius entered her, it seemed as if everything in the universe instantly went into slow motion. It wasn't about who could outfreak the other by bending and twisting in new and innovative ways, but about making love and touching each other's souls.

Lucius's long and deep strokes had tears surfacing and leaking from Beverly's eyes as if she had truly reached the heavens. *What is he doing to me?* Beverly gasped when Lucius's hips dipped and rotated in a hypnotic groove.

"I want to make love like this with you forever," he whispered against her ear. "I want to feel you every morning and taste you just like this every night." Lucius's lips brushed against her shoulders. "Wouldn't you like that?"

Beverly sighed and moaned.

"Hmmm?" His kisses moved to her sensitive neck. "Don't you know how much I've fallen for you, baby? You know how much I love holding you like this. Look at you. You like how I make you feel, don't you?"

"Aaaah," Beverly moaned.

Lucius's strokes slowed even further, causing her to claw impatiently at his back. "You don't love me, Beverly? Is that what you're trying to say?"

"N—no."

As a reward, his hips returned to their previous rhythm. "Do you love me?"

She bit her lips, trying to prevent the truth from spilling.

"I want to hear you say it," he urged. "I know you do. I can feel it." He captured her lips in a long, deep kiss, determined to coax her confession out of her. When he finally came up for air, he asked, "Do you feel it, Beverly?"

A familiar tremble started in her thighs and moved up to the tip of her clit and lower belly. Her breathing became choppy, her defenses lowered.

Lucius dipped his head low, licked at her breasts. "Feel that, Beverly?"

"Y—yes."

His toes tingled. "Damn, I love you, woman." He pulled her legs up and hung them over his shoulders so he could get as deep as he possibly could.

As bliss unfolded from every pore of Beverly's body, she chanted Lucius's name and finally told him what he'd been longing to hear. "I love you, baby."

In what was becoming a habit, after Beverly's third orgasm, she curled up to Lucius and fell asleep. Unfazed, Lucius just smiled and pressed a kiss against her forehead and then gently climbed out of bed and tiptoed to his jacket, which was lying with the rest his clothes on the floor.

When he crept back to the bed, he held in his hand the diamond ring he'd hoped to have given her during dinner. He carefully climbed back into bed, opened the jeweler's burgundy velvet box and plucked out the two-carat, princess-cut diamond ring and prayed like he'd never prayed before that he'd guessed the right size. Quietly, he reached for her right hand, lifted it and slid the platinum band up her ring finger.

Perfect.

Lucius kissed her temple again and curled up against her. He couldn't wait until she woke up and saw the diamond twinkling on her finger. With one more kiss to the back of her head, he closed his eyes and drifted off to sleep.

When he woke up, the bed was empty, but the engagement ring sat gleaming on the pillow next to him. Stunned and heartbroken, he reached for it and belatedly noticed a folded note. Lucius opened it and read the one word scrawled across it. *Sorry.*

Chapter 19

"You did what?" Clarence asked, cupping his ear toward her. "I know I didn't hear you right."

Beverly huffed and rolled her eyes. "I knew that I shouldn't have told you." She stood from her desk and marched out of her office, but she knew good and damn well that it was going to take more than that to get her best friend off her back once she fed him a juicy story.

"Hold up, Bev. Why did you break up with Lucius? You're crazy about the guy."

At the front cash register, Leslie tried to pretend that she wasn't listening to her boss's private conversation.

"C'mon, Clarence. You know why. I promised myself years ago that I didn't want to marry again. And what happened to his promise about a no-strings-attached relationship?" Beverly tossed her hands up in the air. "There are so many strings I feel like I'm choking."

"You don't think that you're exaggerating a bit?"

"No." She wiped at a tear before anyone could see it fall. "And mighty funny Lucius suddenly wants to get married just weeks after he becomes a full-time single father."

"What are you saying?"

Beverly shrugged and said words she didn't believe. "I'm just wondering whether he's really looking for a wife or a new mother for his eight-year-old daughter."

Clarence shoved a hand against his hip. "I ought to wash your mouth out with soap for that."

"What?" she asked defensively. "It's a legitimate question."

"It would be if I didn't see how that man had to practically beg you to go out with him *before* his ex-wife abandoned her daughter with him. You had that boy whipped from day one and you know it. All this other stuff you're saying is extraneous B.S. and you know it." He turned abruptly toward Leslie. "Ain't I right, girl?"

"Well, if you ask me—"

"I'm not asking you," Beverly snapped. "Get back to work."

Clarence jumped to Leslie's defense. "Hey, don't take out all your frustrations on Leslie. You're wrong and you know you're wrong."

"Fine. Maybe I'm just scared then," she said, laying it all out on the line. "What's wrong with that? This whole thing is going at warp speed. A shoe has to drop sooner or later."

"So why not throw your shoe in first?"

"Stop pretending that you don't know what I'm talking about. I can't be a wife again. I can't be that precious little girl's…mother." She choked over that last word. "I just can't."

The shop's doorbell jingled.

Beverly mopped at her eyes, put on a smile and turned to see Tamara Hodges stroll through the door. She blinked. "Oh, my God, Tamara." Her eyes then fell to the small but noticeable bulge of her belly. "You look...wonderful," she announced with amazement and then embraced her for a quick hug.

"You're sweet," Tamara gushed, pulling out of Beverly's arms and glancing around. "What a lovely shop. It's hip and beautiful—so totally you."

"Now who's being sweet?" Beverly winked. "So Kyra told me a couple of weeks ago that you needed an engagement dress?"

Tamara blushed. "Yes. Can you believe it? I'm about to be Mrs. Micah Ross."

"Oooh." Once again, Clarence hip-bumped his way into the small circle. "*You're* the one marrying that gorgeous music mogul?"

Smiling, Tamara blinked at Beverly's overzealous friend. "I take it you've heard of him."

"Who hasn't it? Giirrll, let me see the ring!" He didn't wait for her to do it on her own. Instead, he grabbed her hand and then faked a heart attack when he saw it. "Chile, is that a ring or a small planet?"

Delighted with his theatrics, Tamara laughed. "It is beautiful, isn't it?"

"I'd say." He glanced over at Beverly. "'Tis the season for brothers to be passing out diamond rings."

"What?" Tamara asked, confused.

"Don't mind him." Beverly moved around Clarence and gently directed Tamara away. "Why don't you just tell me what kind of dress you had in mind...?"

* * *

Lucius was angry.

Despite this, he put on a brave face so his daughter could enjoy the Christmas holidays. The last three days were particularly hard with Ruby constantly asking when Beverly was coming back over—which was remarkable since she hardly mentioned her own mother.

Balancing work, home and the approaching holiday had Lucius feeling like he was burning the candle at both ends. However, at night he relished the exhaustion. It was the only thing to help him sleep through the night. Yet, it was the first few minutes upon waking that really got to him. He missed the mornings when he'd awakened curled like a spoon against Beverly's curvy bottle shape. If he concentrated, he could still recall the coconut scent in her hair.

Lucius's heart ached while he waited for his alarm clock to tell him to get out of bed. Until then, he easily pulled up Beverly's angelic face from memory and recounted everything he loved about it. At exactly 5:30 a.m., he flung out an arm and shut off the alarm's loud and annoying buzz. However, he didn't climb out of bed. Instead he remained nestled in his white cotton sheets, staring up at the ceiling.

Lucius huffed, rolled over onto his side and stared at the clock. Its loud ticking sounded as if it was hooked up into an amplifier. In no time his heart and the muscles along his temples thumped in precise harmony.

Maybe he should just stay in bed today.

"Daddy! Daddy!" Ruby bolted into his room, hopped up onto the bed and started shaking his shoulders. "Daddy, it's time to get up."

He groaned. Why did he have the child that sprang out of bed in the mornings? He rolled over and couldn't help but laugh at the sight of her hair sticking up all over the place. "I'm getting up, sweetheart." He reached out and mussed her hair up even more. "What do you want for breakfast?"

"Waffles!"

He rolled his eyes because her answer came as no surprise. "All righty," he said, peeling back the top sheet and climbing out of bed. "Waffles it is!"

In the kitchen, Lucius endured another long line of hard-hitting questions about Beverly's whereabouts and whether he thought that she was mad at them.

"Maybe you should just call her and apologize," Ruby said.

"What makes you think that *I* did something wrong?"

This time his little girl made eyes at him as though he'd asked a dumb question. "C'mon, Daddy. You're a boy."

It was on the tip of his tongue to ask what the heck that meant, but Lucius feared she would actually have an answer. "Let's just say it's a little more complicated than that, sweetie."

The toaster popped up their waffles and Lucius quickly placed them on their plates and grabbed a bottle of syrup.

"Daddy, can we go shopping tomorrow?" Ruby asked, cutting into her food. "I want to buy Beverly a Christmas present."

Once again Lucius weighed whether he should go ahead and tell her that Beverly was likely never coming around again, but when he looked into her eager hazel eyes, he just couldn't get himself to say the words. "We'll see, sweetie. We'll see."

* * *

Beverly played with her cereal while allowing the house's silence to cloak her. She had long ago lost count of how many times she'd looked at her finger and recalled how that beautiful ring Lucius gave her had sparkled on her hand. Then, like now, tears had rushed to her eyes and her heart ached for something she'd long told herself that she didn't want.

Yet after three days that fear was being replaced by another. The fear of living the rest of her life in this house…alone.

She pushed her bowl away and marched out of her kitchen to go get dressed. As she shuffled up the stairs, a familiar icy cold lifted an army of goose bumps along her arms and caused her hackles to rise. At the top of the stairs, Beverly's gaze immediately went to that closed door at the end of the hallway.

I really should get ready for work, she told herself, but her feet were already carrying her toward the forbidden door. The knob was cold, as usual, but today, she opened the door anyway. From the moment she saw the blue walls, her vision blurred and tears snaked from her eyes.

The room hadn't changed in five years. Her gaze shifted from the Spider-Man sheets on the twin-size bed to the mass of action figures crammed in a clear plastic tub next to the window. That familiar sense of injustice bubbled up inside of her. She walked over to the bed and eased down onto the edge, but it wasn't long before she was blinded by the seemingly endless stream of tears of a mother who'd lost her child.

Chapter 20

With it being Christmas Eve, Lucius planned only to put in a couple of hours at work. There was another major litigation case coming around the bend and he was already worried about how he was going to juggle it all given his new responsibilities at home. "Where there's a will, there's a way," he muttered under his breath.

However, his butt had hardly hit his chair a full minute before Maggie was buzzing in over the speakerphone. "Mr. Gray, I have Mitch Paulson here to see you."

He frowned at the phone and then punched in a few keystrokes on his computer.

"He doesn't have an appointment," she said, answering his unspoken question.

Annoyed but knowing how valuable the boisterous businessman was to his company, Lucius instructed Maggie to send him on in.

Paulson strolled through the door; his bulky six-six frame shrank the room around him. It was just eight o'clock in the morning and the large cowboy was already puffing on a thick cigar and looking like he was ready for his morning brandy. "I knew that you'd be in the office today," he said, cocking his hand like a gun and firing an invisible shot.

"Just for a couple of hours," Lucius assured him and then gestured to the chair in front of his desk. "Have a seat."

"Don't mind if I do." Paulson chuckled and folded into the chair with a slight grunt.

"Now what can I do you for?" Lucius asked, returning to his own chair.

"Well, I want to sue the government," the Texan announced.

"Again?" Lucius asked with a wry smile.

"Well, they're always pissing me off," he said simply.

Lucius chuckled. "Well, what did the government do this time?"

"I'm suing for their abuse of eminent domain," Paulson huffed.

Braiding his fingers together, he listened patiently to his lawsuit-addicted client. His case this time sounded no more convincing than the legion of others that Kendall, Hendrix and Gray, LLC had worked on for the brash Texan. For the most part, they were willing to kill as many trees as Paulson wanted as long as Paulson was willing to write checks.

"Well, I'll certainly jump right on it," Lucius assured Paulson when he finished his long spiel. He stood and offered the man his hand. "I should have some preliminary paperwork for you to review by next week."

Paulson winked. "I knew I could count on you." He

accepted Lucius's handshake. "By the way, whatever happened with you and that hot tamale at the bar a couple of months ago?"

Lucius stiffened as his hand fell away, but he quickly recovered and tried to shrug off the question. "Aww. Well. You know. You win some, you lose some."

"Is that right?" Paulson's thick salt-and-pepper brows crashed together as his gaze seemed to look at Lucius as if he was made of glass. "Hmmm. When I saw you two at Ruth's Chris Steak House a few nights ago, I thought you'd struck a love connection—judging by the way you were looking at her." His statement shaved a few inches off Lucius's plastic smile.

Instead of remaining evasive, Lucius came clean. "I thought so, too."

"She dumped you?"

"I guess you can say that," Lucius answered, despite being uncomfortable by the line of questioning.

"Aww. Damn. That's too bad." Paulson chomped on his cigar. "I was sort of hoping that at least one of us could get a second chance at something a little more meaningful than…" He glanced around the room. "Than the spoils of success. You know my motto—A Career Is Great, But a Woman Is Better."

"I remember you saying something like that."

Paulson continued to read him. "It was the hours—"

"No. No." Lucius shook his head, amazed that he *wanted* to talk about this. "Believe it or not, my job had nothing to do with it. I guess we should have just remained two ships passing in the middle of the night."

"I hear what you're saying but you sound like a man barely held together with tape. Do you love this girl?"

Lucius hesitated. "I thought I did."

Paulson cocked his head and waited a little longer for the truth. "I do. Madly. Deeply."

"Then what the hell are you doing here?"

Lucius dropped back into his chair and exhaled a long, frustrated sigh. "Because our love apparently is a one-way street."

"You sure about that?"

"Pretty sure. I call myself being romantic by sliding an engagement ring on her finger while she was sleeping, thinking I'd wake to smiles and kisses. Instead I woke to an empty bed—except for the ring and a note."

Paulson grimaced. "Ouch."

"That's putting it mildly."

"What'd the note say?"

Lucius shrugged. "Sorry."

"I mean you don't have to tell me if you don't want to."

"No. I mean that's what the note said. 'Sorry.'"

"A woman of few words."

Lucius nodded and then reflected over the events from the past several months. "Maybe I rushed her. I know she still has a few scars left from her first marriage. The whole time, she tried to keep me at arm's length, but I thought I was breaking down her defenses. In fact, I would have staked my life on it."

"Maybe you did." Paulson removed the cigar from his mouth. "What did she say when you talked to her?"

Lucius pulled out of his reverie. "I haven't seen her since."

"You're kidding me, right?"

Lucius looked up. Shrugged.

"I thought you said you loved this girl? You're going to just go down without a fight?"

Frowning, Lucius shifted uncomfortably in his seat. "What do you mean?"

Paulson started laughing. "C'mon. You're a man of the world. Surely you know anything worth having is worth fighting for. You love the woman, you fight for her. Assure her that you're nothing like the creep that broke her heart. You keep at it until you convince her—that or until she issues a restraining order—whichever comes first."

"What are you, Dr. Phil now?"

"He's not the only Texan that knows how to dole out common sense."

Lucius laughed.

"Okay. All jokes aside, son. If you really want her, you're going to have to fight for her."

Hoops was crowded with last-minute Christmas shoppers. Lucius took a deep breath to try to calm his nerves, but there was nothing he could do about the large lump bobbing in the center of his throat. After talking to Paulson, he'd felt like a complete idiot for not realizing what he needed to do sooner. Of course, Beverly was still gun-shy about walking down the aisle again. How many times had he seen that fear up close and personal, especially at Hollington's class reunion?

Looking back, he knew that his proposal was all wrong. He needed to look Beverly in the eye and assure her that he was nothing like David Clark. He needed to address her fears one by one and then make it clear that he was willing to wait for as long as she wanted him. Instead, he had allowed his pride to prevent him from seeing what was perfectly obvious.

"Excuse me," he repeated to one woman after another as he threaded his way toward the front cash register.

Behind the counter there was only one face he recognized. "Um, Leslie, right?"

The young lady's eyes rounded wide with surprise. "Lucius…I mean, Mr. Gray. You finally came."

He frowned. "Were you expecting me?"

"Sort of." She quickly scooped a cell phone out her pants pocket.

Lucius frowned. "Um, is Beverly here?"

Leslie held up a slender finger and punched in a few numbers. "Clarence, he's here." Pause. "Okay." She disconnected the call. "He's on his way over."

"Clarence?" Why on earth would she think he wanted to speak to him? "Is Beverly here?" he asked again.

"No. Sorry. She never made it in this morning."

He frowned, wondering whether there was a problem. He turned to leave, but was surprised when he ran smack into Clarence. *How in the hell did he get here so fast?*

"Good. I caught you," Clarence said, panting. "It certainly took you long enough to show up."

"Is there a problem?"

"The only problem I see is that my best friend is trying to throw away her best chance for happiness." He folded his arms. "You do intend to try and make her happy, don't you?"

"If she'll let me."

Clarence eyeballed him a little longer and then finally said, "Come with me."

Lucius frowned, but followed the strutting man to the back of the store. At the small employee break table, Clarence told him to take a seat. Curious, he did what he was told and then waited.

"Beverly is at home," Clarence started.

Lucius jumped to his feet.

"But before you go flying over there I think I need to arm you with a little information."

Now Clarence had his undivided attention. He sat back down and leaned back in the small metal chair and crossed his arms. "I'm listening."

It rarely snowed in Atlanta and to have that rare phenomenon occur on Christmas Eve had to be something like a billion-to-one odds. Still, it gave Lucius the feeling that he was driving through a magical snow globe. When he pulled into the driveway leading toward Beverly's house, he was once again hit by how lonely and sad the house appeared—and now he knew why.

He parked the car and climbed out of the vehicle. For a few seconds he stood outside just staring at the house. The cold and sadness permeated his bones and chilled his soul. Finally, he strolled up to the door, rang the doorbell and waited. Around him, the snow thickened, transforming the place to look like a whimsical painting.

After a few minutes, it was clear that Beverly wasn't coming to the door. He turned toward a large potted plant, tilted it over and retrieved the key that Clarence told him Beverly kept there for emergencies.

Lucius slipped the key into the lock and then slowly entered the house. "Beverly?" he called out, closing the door behind him.

The house roared with silence. He started to check downstairs, but something told him that she was more likely to be upstairs. "Beverly, sweetheart?" he called again as he ascended.

It wasn't until he reached the top stair that he heard the soft whimpers. His eyes immediately zoomed to the cracked door at the end of the hallway. On autopilot, he moved toward the heart-wrenching sobs, trying to prepare himself for what he might find on the other side. Placing his hand on the door, he gently pushed it open farther.

Beverly sat hunched over on the small twin-size bed, holding a large picture frame and rocking back and forth. It took a second, but she stopped and slowly lifted her tear-filled eyes. "It's not that I don't love you," she said in a quivering voice as if they were picking up on an unfinished conversation. "I do. Lord knows I do despite my trying to fight it. But…"

Lucius walked over to the bed while she struggled to collect herself. He knelt down in front of her and reached for the picture she held in her arms. "May I see him?"

Beverly released the frame and then watched Lucius's face when he looked down at Gregory William Clark.

"He was a handsome boy. How old was he in this picture?"

"Five," she said with a nostalgic smile. "It was taken maybe three months before he was diagnosed with cancer. He had acute lymphoblastic leukemia. We spent a full year fighting that disease and then…it was just over. His little body couldn't take it." She feverishly wiped at her tears. "At first, I was so glad that he no longer had to endure all of that pain and suffering. But then I started missing all those smiles and hugs that he was always trying to give out."

Lucius stared at the handsome boy that looked more like his mother than his father and his heart broke for what the world had lost.

"For a year, I lived in Egleston Children Hospital, reading him stories, mopping his fevered brow. David…" Beverly sniffed and then shook her head. "Let's just say our marriage was on life support after Gregory passed away. David seemed to think I could just snap my fingers and be over it—apparently, it worked for him." She shrugged. "Two years later he had an affair and then we got a divorce." She sighed. "It was all a pathetic tragedy—one I vowed that I would never repeat."

Lucius looked up and met her steady gaze.

Beverly continued. "I did everything—medication, therapy. The only thing that worked was when I convinced myself to build a wall around my heart and just bury myself in my work." She smiled tenderly as she reached out and stroked his face. "And then you came along...and then your beautiful daughter. Suddenly I was part of a family again...and I loved it."

Lucius grabbed hold of her hand and kissed it. "Ruby and I both love having you as a part of our lives," he said. "And we want you back."

"I'm sorry I ran out on you. I know I promised never to do that again, but..." She broke eye contact to glance around the room. "I should have told you about Gregory sooner."

"You needed more time," he said, understanding.

"A little," she agreed. "But now I know it's way past time for me to let go—time for me to sell this place and move on." Beverly's gaze found his again. She searched through the windows of his soul and saw nothing but love.

"I'm not David," he said. "I'll never let you go through anything by yourself. I promise to love and support you through thick and thin. I give you my word."

She leaned forward and brushed a feathery light kiss against his lips. Suddenly, in this gloomy room, hope had penetrated. "I know you will. And I promise you that I'll love and support you through thick and thin, too. And I promise I'll be a good stepmother to your little girl."

Lucius's smile widened before he leaned closer for a stronger, deeper kiss. "I love you."

"I love you, too."

Reaching into his pocket, Lucius pulled out the burgundy velvet box and popped open the lid. To his surprise his hand trembled as he removed the platinum ring nestled in the center. "Beverly Turner, will you do me the great honor of becoming my wife?"

"Yes." She bobbed her head while tears streamed down her face. She watched as Lucius slid the engagement ring back onto her finger—where it belonged.

Smiling, he swept Beverly up into his arms and carried her out of her son's old room. "Where's your bedroom?"

"Down the hall, last door on your right," she whispered.

As he walked their gazes remained locked, and without words their eyes said so much. In her bedroom, Lucius laid her gently onto the bed and kissed her so tenderly that a new wave of tears crested and slid from the corners of her eyes. From his lips she tasted true love. What few doubts she had about walking down the aisle again melted away. In her head, she could already see what their forever entailed: their businesses growing, their family expanding and their love never-ending.

Lucius took his time peeling away her clothes. His eyes, as well as his touch, made love to her in ways that were just mind-blowing. When their bodies joined, Beverly realized that everything that she'd ever gone through, good and bad, was meant to lead her to this perfect moment.

As their bodies moved in time to a rhythm only their hearts could hear, Beverly made sure that she reciprocated all that she was feeling. After her orgasm hit and left her panting, she had a hard time discerning exactly where her body ended and where his began. Then again, it didn't matter. From this day on, they would live and breathe as one.

Watching as love and pleasure ebbed and flowed across Beverly's beautiful face, Lucius felt his heart swell. He looked forward to making love to this woman for the rest of his life. As sure as he breathed, he knew that there was nothing he wouldn't do to keep Beverly at his side— forever and always.

Ruby woke up Christmas morning to what she declared was the best Christmas surprise ever: Beverly sitting next to the large Christmas tree in the living room. "Beverly, you're back!" Ruby actually bypassed the large, pretty decorative boxes and launched herself into Beverly's arms, overwhelming her with hugs and kisses.

"Of course I'm back. I couldn't stay away from my favorite girl for long."

Lucius entered the room, carrying a tray of hot chocolate and beaming at his two favorite girls. Just then Ruby noticed the sparkling diamond on Beverly's hand. "You're wearing Daddy's ring!" Her head jerked from Beverly to her father. "Does that mean she's going to marry us, Daddy?"

Lucius set the tray down on the coffee table, folded one arm across his chest while his free hand stroked his chin as he contemplated the question. "Hmmm. That's a very good question." His sparkling gaze at long last settled on his daughter. "Why don't you ask her?"

Ruby was only too happy to comply. "Beverly, are you going to marry us?"

Beverly laughed as tears rose and skipped over her lashes. "I most certainly am."

"Yay!" Ruby's arms flew back around Beverly's neck, almost choking her.

"All right. All right," Lucius said, coming to Beverly's rescue when he saw how her eyes bugged out. "Time to dig into these Christmas gifts."

As if finally remembering what day it was, Ruby released her death grip and sprang out of Beverly's lap to jet over to the tree. For the next three hours Beverly and Lucius sat curled up on the sofa, watching Ruby tear through the boxes like a Tasmanian devil, squealing at every large *and* small gift.

The whole scene felt like a special Christmas fairy tale to Beverly, but she only had to look to the man sitting beside her to know that it was all so very real. It was hard to believe that just a couple of months ago she didn't know this wonderful man, and now she couldn't imagine a life without him. Who would have ever thought that a simple college reunion would have changed her life? And she wasn't the only one. Chloe and Kevin, Tamara and Micah, and even Kyra and Terrence had all found or rediscovered love.

Lucius looked up from the beautiful watch she'd given him, then narrowed his gaze in suspicion. "What are you thinking so hard about?"

"Hollington," Beverly answered. "I think this year we owe them a *big* donation."

He leaned over and kissed her. "I couldn't agree with you more."

Epilogue

Six months later

There's a reason June is the perfect time for weddings in Georgia. And on this midsummer evening the sun was setting, the air was moist and a light breeze carried the wonderful sweet scent of magnolias. With everything being so perfect, Beverly was sure that at any moment someone was going to wake her up and tell her that the past eight months had been nothing but a dream. Yet after giving herself several pinches on the arm, she finally accepted that this day was very much real.

Her three smiling bridesmaids—Chloe, Tamara and Kyra—had gushed over her first handmade white-and-silver beaded wedding dress and even managed to fill her head with ideas of perhaps starting her own wedding-gown line. Beverly appreciated the praise, but knew her friends were working overtime in trying to soothe her nervousness about taking her second trip down the aisle.

It was a big step…and one that she was wholeheartedly committed to making.

Her nervousness didn't stem from any questions of her love for Lucius. Far from it. In fact, she didn't even think it was possible to love him any more than she did right now. He was her knight in shining armor who had most assuredly rescued her from a future of bitter loneliness. And he had confessed that she had rescued him from the same fate. Nowadays, most of their friends and family had teased them about not being able to keep their hands off each other or how effortlessly they finished each other's thoughts and sentences.

Her nervous jitters came solely from her fierce desire to be the best wife and mother Lucius wanted and needed her to be.

"Stop worrying," Beverly's mother whispered in her ear, mere minutes before she needed to rush out to her seat. "You picked a winner this time."

Beverly's cherry-red smile stretched across her face. It absolutely warmed her heart that this time around, her parents approved of her choice for a husband. And of course they simply adored Ruby, but who didn't? Ruby with her warm smile and infectious laughter had taken to Beverly becoming her stepmother like a fish to water.

But Ruby had her melancholy days—especially when Erica reappeared shortly after New Year's with a change of heart, wanting Ruby back. Lucius's patience with his ex had finally snapped. He'd had enough of the games and had hauled Erica's butt into court for full custody. Enough was enough. As a result, Ruby had her good days and her bad days, but Beverly and Lucius worked overtime to make sure Ruby knew without a doubt that she was wanted and very much loved.

When the wedding planner signaled for everyone to take their places, Beverly's heart kicked up a couple of notches.

"You look faint," Clarence said, alarmed. "I'm going to get you some water." Without waiting for a response, he raced out of the room while Chloe, Tamara and Kyra aided her in taking a seat.

Chloe grabbed a leaflet from a nearby nightstand and began fanning it profusely in Beverly's face. "Honey, are you sure you're all right?"

The cool breeze was just what Beverly needed. "Yes. Yes. I'll be fine."

Tamara's perceptive gaze narrowed into a squint. "I hope I'm not being too nosy, but…are you pregnant?"

Beverly blushed.

Her bridesmaids gasped, then squealed with delight.

"I can't believe you didn't tell me!" Kyra admonished with a dramatic stomp of her foot, but in the next second swept her friend into her arms while still being careful not to muss her up too much.

"When did you find out?" Chloe asked, her own pregnancy clearly evident. No one doubted that Chloe and Kevin were extremely happy. The three-month newlyweds couldn't keep their hands off each other either. And there was no wonder. Chloe's pregnancy had transformed her from a subtle beauty to a dynamic one. Everyone noticed her now whenever she walked into a room. Her black hair shone, her flawless skin glowed. It was a wonder to all who knew her now how she could ever have been a silent wall-flower.

Tamara had had a similar transformation. Still a newly-wed herself, her body had gone through a few minor changes, too. Bigger breasts equaled a happier husband. That is, whenever Micah junior felt like sharing. So far, Tamara and her husband split their time between Los Angeles and Atlanta, but it was looking more and more as if the small family would settle down out west.

Beverly continued to blush like a prepubescent teenager as she finally answered Chloe's question. "Three days."

There was more gasping and squealing.

"Does Lucius know?" Chloe asked, wide-eyed.

"No." Beverly shook her head. "I'm planning to make the announcement at the reception."

"Oh, my God." Tamara clasped Beverly's hand. "He's going to be thrilled!"

"I know." Beverly bubbled.

"Who's going to be thrilled about what?" Clarence asked, returning to the bridal suite with a pitcher of ice water.

Chloe opened her mouth to fill Clarence in on Beverly's surprise, but Beverly quickly grabbed her friend by the wrist to catch her attention, then silently shook her head.

"What's this?" Clarence set the pitcher down on a table and folded his arms. "Why do I smell a secret in the air?"

"No offense, Clarence," Beverly said, flashing him a kind smile. "But if we tell you, then it won't be a secret anymore."

Clarence gasped and spread a hand across his heart. "What? Girl, you know I can keep a secret. Okay…so I've dropped dime on a few things from time to time." He shrugged. "But I promise—whatever it is, I'll keep my mouth shut."

Beverly shook her head. "Sorry."

Clarence poked out his bottom lip and hit her with his huge puppy-dog eyes.

"Not going to work."

The wedding planner slipped her head back into the suite. "What are you all still doing in here? Places! We're on in *two* minutes."

The bridal party scrambled.

Clarence sputtered after Beverly, "But—but—"

Lucius waited at the outdoor altar next to the preacher with his heart lodged in the middle of his throat. A few more guests hurried to their seats. Lucius smiled, then his attention shifted when the music started. Ruby, the flower girl in an adorable white-and-silver dress, strolled down the aisle next to her four-year-old cousin Alan, the official ring bearer.

Halfway down the aisle Alan decided he wanted to go and sit next to his parents and had to be coaxed back to finish his walk to Lucius's side. The whole episode was adorable and had the guests laughing. However, minutes later the bridesmaids walked arm in arm with the grooms-men—who in this case were their recent husbands.

Mr. and Mrs. Kevin and Chloe Stayton.

Mr. and Mrs. Micah and Tamara Ross.

Mr. and Mrs. Terrence and Kyra Franklin.

And then Clarence, the man of honor, and the best man, Mitch Paulson, made their way down the aisle—an unlikely duo, to say the least. But the broad-shouldered Texan seemed to take it all in stride. Clarence worked the aisle like a mini two-step fashion runway. But he reeled it in at the last moment and took his place next to the bridesmaids.

At last the music changed. Lucius straightened his back as the moment he'd been waiting for finally arrived. Beverly made her grand entrance while hooked on the arm of her father.

She was a stunning vision and completely stole his breath away. Lucius was overwhelmed by his love toward his approaching bride—a love so strong that it both frightened and awed him at the same time. When she stopped before him and smiled, it felt as if his heart was literally melting and pooling at her feet.

Together they turned toward the preacher. Lucius could barely pay attention to what was being said once Beverly stopped beside him. All that kept flooding through his mind were all the possibilities that their future held. When it came time for the wedding vows, Ruby moved to stand next to him and together they recited the words they had written together. Perfect pearl-shaped tears glided down Beverly's beautiful face as she said her own memorized vows to Lucius. At long last, their love was proclaimed and sealed with a kiss.

"Ladies and gentlemen," the preacher said. "May I present to you Mr. and Mrs. Lucius and Beverly Gray."

Their guests cheered as they tossed out a mixed shower of roses and confetti at the beautiful couple. Minutes later, everyone milled over to the reception hall. Beverly and

Lucius kept their hands and lips locked together for most of the time. After the speeches from the man of honor and the best man, Beverly knew that it was time to make her big announcement. A vat of butterflies filled her belly as she took the microphone from Clarence and stood from the table.

"I have an announcement I'd like to make."

Curious, Lucius looked up and watched his nervous wife. *Wife.* He loved the sound of that.

Beverly took a deep breath. "First I'd like to say that Lucius and I are very grateful that all of you could come today and be a part of this beautiful wedding." She smiled broadly, then took another breath.

Sensing that she needed a little encouragement, Lucius reached for her hand again and squeezed.

Beverly's smile grew brighter as she turned toward him and met his loving gaze with her own. "What I have to announce will even be news to my adoring husband."

Lucius's brows rose in surprise.

"Honey," Beverly began while her eyes misted, "we're pregnant."

Lucius's jaw dropped while the wedding party once again cheered enthusiastically. In the next second Lucius jumped to his feet and swept Beverly into his arms. "Oh, my God, baby. Are you sure? This in incredible."

Beverly bobbed her head as tears streamed from her eyes.

Moments later Clarence announced that it was time for the couple's first dance. Lucius offered his wife his arm, then led her to the floor just as Lauryn Hill's "Sweetest Thing" began to play. Beverly and Lucius smiled into each other's eyes. They were the happiest people on earth.

The wedding party remained an adoring captive audience throughout the dance and when the song ended the crowd rewarded them with applause. Clarence stood with the microphone while wiping tears from his eyes. "Y'all just don't know what my girl Leslie and I went through to get these two together."

Leslie waved from one of the tables.

"Now," Clarence continued, "we want to invite the following newlyweds to join our loving couple on the dance floor. Chloe and Kevin Stayton, Tamara and Micah Ross and Kyra and Terrence Franklin."

The crowd applauded again while Clarence continued, "For those who don't know, all four couples you see on the floor now met or reunited at their college reunion last year."

Another round of applause.

"So let that be a lesson for you all to show up when you get those pesky invitations in the mail."

The crowd laughed.

"For the next song we invited R & B sensation Justice Kane to transport you all back to that fateful reunion weekend," Clarence boasted. "Enjoy."

Justice Kane took the microphone and launched into his hit song "Tender to His Touch."

Lucius's arm tightened around Beverly. "In case I haven't told you today, I love you, Mrs. Gray."

"And I love you, Mr. Gray. Forever and ever."

He leaned in for a long, tender kiss. "I'm going to hold you to that, my love."

Her smile ballooned. "That's what I was hoping for, my love."

Lucius's smile matched her own. "Say that again."

"My love," she whispered and delivered another kiss. "My love. My love. My love."

* * * * *

REQUEST YOUR FREE BOOKS!

2 FREE NOVELS
PLUS 2 FREE GIFTS!

KIMANI™
ROMANCE

Love's ultimate destination!

Essence **Bestselling Author**

GWYNNE FORSTER

Out of affection and loneliness, Melinda Rodgers married a wealthy older man. Now a widow at twenty-nine, she must remarry within the year or lose her inheritance.

As executor, handsome Blake Hunter insists Melinda carry out the will's terms. And judging by the dangerous, unfulfilled yearning that's simmered between them for years, Blake may be the man to bring her the most passionate kind of love… or the most heartbreaking betrayal.

SCARLET WOMAN

"A delightful book romance lovers will enjoy."
—*RT Book Reviews* on *Once in a Lifetime*

Coming the first week of December 2009 wherever books are sold.

www.kimanipress.com
www.myspace.com/kimanipress

KPGF1691209

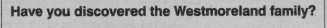

HELP CELEBRATE
ARABESQUE'S
15TH ANNIVERSARY!

2009 marks Arabesque's 15th anniversary!

Help us celebrate by telling us about your most special memories and moments with Arabesque books. Entries will be judged by the Arabesque Anniversary Committee based on which are the most touching and well written. Fifteen lucky winners will receive as a prize a full-grain leather duffel bag with the Arabesque anniversary logo.

How to Enter: To enter, hand-print (or type) on an 8 ½" x 11" plain piece of paper your full name, mailing address, telephone number and a description of your most special memories and moments with Arabesque books (in two hundred [200] words or less) and send it to "Arabesque 15th Anniversary Contest 20901"—in the U.S.: Kimani Press, 233 Broadway, Suite 1001, New York, NY 10279, or in Canada: 225 Duncan Mill Road, Don Mills, ON M3B 3K9. No other method of entry will be accepted. The contest begins on July 1, 2009, and ends on December 31, 2009. Entries must be postmarked by December 31, 2009, and received by January 8, 2010. A copy of these Official Rules is available online at www.myspace.com/kimanipress, or to obtain a copy of these Official Rules (prior to November 30, 2009), send a self-addressed, stamped envelope (postage not required from residents of VT) to "Arabesque 15th Anniversary Contest 20901 Rules," 225 Duncan Mill Road, Don Mills, ON M3B 3K9. Limit one (1) entry per person. If more than one (1) entry is received from the same person, only the first eligible entry submitted will be considered. By entering the contest, entrants agree to be bound by these Official Rules and the decisions of Harlequin Enterprises Limited (the "Sponsor"), which are final and binding.

NO PURCHASE NECESSARY. Open to legal residents of U.S. and Canada (except Quebec) who have reached the age of majority at time of entry. Void where prohibited by law. Approximate retail value of each prize: $131.00 (USD).

VISIT **WWW.MYSPACE.COM/KIMANIPRESS**
FOR THE COMPLETE OFFICIAL RULES

KPISARACONTEST